The
SISTERS
of
CYNVAEL

DIANA POWELL

Published by Liquorice Fish Books
an imprint of Cinnamon Press,
Office 49019, PO Box 15113, Birmingham, B2 2NJ
www.cinnamonpress.com

Print Edition ISBN 978-1-911540-20-5
Ebook Edition ISBN 978-1-911540-27-4

British Library Cataloguing in Publication Data. A CIP record for this book can be obtained from the British Library.

Cover and interior designed and typeset by Adam Craig/Liquorice Fish Books.

Liquorice Fish Books is represented by Inpress.

The
SISTERS
of
CYNVAEL

'A-fon', 'Cyn-vael'. Hear it.

Hear the river, hear the word.

Say it—rivvaaa. Roll it round your tongue, rolling like the…

River. *My* river. Lullaby, nag. Friend, foe. Shape-shifter.

Shifting flud, bourn; ceffyl y dwr, millpond. Spit, splash, plash, JUMPS, JUMPS, JUMPS, rattles down the mountain, snakes, rushes, dawdles, as it drags its arms behind, smirking… Lording (ladying?), at what it leaves behind.

Waters broke, birthed me, my mother says. Here. Seen from our window, a stone's throw, a girl's languished arrow. *There*, if true. So…

the river birthed me, birthed this place. Coming down from the mountain, scritching bit by bit, the rock, the earth. Eating it, you could say, a maiden's prissy mouthful at a time. Then gorging over what it had done.

'This is how a valley is formed,' he said, pedant's cap on, always schooling, wanting us to know, burbling words the way the winter-spring gushes. 'Look.' 'See.' 'Here.' Blah, blah, blah. Showing us lines in the rocks by the Fall, squished together, stretched apart; drawing a picture in the muddy bank with his rod of rowan, 'narrow, getting wider, all the way to the sea.' A 'V'. A wedge.

Valley, cwm, River's cradle, River's child, given the same name. Cynvael. The wood, too, though that was later, yet still in ancient times; oak sprung first, king, queen, father, mother of the forest (choose as you like), ash, alder following, gathering to feed from the stream below, elbows jostling for best seat in the house. The house, too, later still, much, much later—our house, the house made by him, stone by stone, him and his brother, my uncle, Owen. Stones carried from the mountain, picked up from the fields, cast there by the giants, the 'hen wr llwyd o'r cornel' and the knitting dames like to say. *Here*—the river, the valley, the wood, the house, us, in this place where they call you by your house/farm name. Jenkin Tŷ Onnen, Jones Tŷ Gwyn. Him, more than that, more than any of those. Him, the Master, the 'Master of Cynvael'. Maybe…

The word: me, my sister, fidgeting in bed beneath our prickly sheep-shorn/home-spun-mother-made blankets, hidden. Me, pointing between my legs. 'Cyn'. The triangle there, a 'V', a wedge. Giggling, then. Her listening, *then*. 'Two peas in a pod/two knives in a sheath/yr un sbit/llathen o'r un brethyn.'
Before we were wedged apart.
Him.
Our father. Our father which art in Heaven. Is he?

'Put your hands, scrunched to your ears.' Still you'll hear it. Not the blood in your veins, the trickster shell, spat from the sea, fooling by the seashore, two rivers down. Where you went, once. 'Hark!' Not that. This is real. The sound still there, the soft sough caught behind your fingers. Still there, as you lie in that bed, or as you break your fast, or as you throw open the casement, or step outside the door. Louder, closer, closer as you get. From waking to dream-time—there, too, along with brides of flowers, silver moon-goddesses, lost heads. The bride following it—'fast, Blodeuwedd, faster, you and your virgins, hurry, before they catch you'; the goddess rising above it, Arianrhod, silvering, slivering its surface; the heads found by the fall.

Up, down, gushhhhhhhhh. Purrrrl. T...rilllll! An accompaniment. Your music.

Put your hands to your head to block *his* noise. Block his words, chanted, shouted, indulged, those spouted words, spurting out of his mouth, pouring all over you. No need. The river does it for you. Listen to the river, instead. Cynvael.

Thank you, River.

In the beginning... in the beginning, it was different. 'Once upon a time' I liked to hear him—his crooning, lulling, his mouthing my name, his once-upon-a-times, as he looked down upon me, cradle-boxed and wrapped. His gift. I liked to see him, then, his face, the chuckling cheeks; his eyes, seeing them light up at his seeing—me, as he held me in his arms, his only daughter. No Lizzie then, no-one else to judge by, to favour. Just me. So yes, I was smiled upon, kissed, cwtched, all of those pleasures, for days, weeks, months, the first of my life. Happy with him, then; him, happy with me. Until... what?

Day came, when I was taken—in his arms again—to the pool beneath the Falls, further along the river. Rhaeadr Ddu; Pwll Ddu, the Black Pool, not a place for infant coddling, swaddling, swaddled in a muslin shawl, pulled away as he held me, bare, above the water.

My first memory, too young to be remembered, yet I swear there he was, ready to baptise me—me, watching him making the sign of the cross on my forehead, wanting to mark me for the Godhead there and then. For Ever. And Ever, Amen. A line down, a line breaking it, the dribble of the water, the rilled drag of his fingertip, or...

... the Cynvael, licking me, the tip of its tongue, seeking, wanting, pushing this new God away so soon! I felt it there, I smiled, choosing, at that moment, the river's higher claim. Glad, when he lowered his arms, lowered me, under the surface.

But not quite at once.

The shock of it, first! Breath, air gone, what I had grown used to, forgetting the water of my mother's womb, forgetting my rumoured birthing. Where was I? What was this? My river, from beneath, its water sloshing all around me, into me, into my ears, my nose, my open mouth. My mouth open from the shock, from my infant wailing. But the river, Cynvael, taught me, straight away, shutting my lips, telling me to hold my air close, inside me, tight, while it rocked me in its pleated flow.

Safe, now, I looked around, saw velvet-green motes cloud from the bottom, shucked by silver fish, puckering among the weeds—the tendrils of the weeds waving in the current, waving at me, 'hello!', the fish blinking at me through their tattered curtains, all welcoming me home. I saw the grit, the shingle, like chipped gemstones, snug between the rocks snagged from the mountain, brought down, though I didn't know it then, he hadn't told me, in the making of the valley; brought down, since, from the force of its falling. The legs of little-lady-wash-dish, the tip of its tail, as it puttered on the stones above, trying to keep its feet clean; the beak of the dipper as it dipped, bowing, bobbing, searching for grubs. An eyelid of blue, the kingfisher's dive, the silver fish caught. All these lives I saw.

Other images, too, those that peopled my dreams, not knowing, then, that I had dreamed them; not knowing if a child that young can dream. It is just how it seemed.

Pale feet splashing through the stream lower down, bearing the flower girl and her entourage up the mountain. Leather boots following, sending the water flying, the women flying. A stone, half-buried in the depths, riven by a spear, the spear falling. A body, falling, the spear through it, tendrils of blood, now, seeping towards me.

All these sights I think I saw. In the river.

Cynvael, River. Mine. No. Other way around.

It licked me more; its tongue, this time, slicked, slobbery, spittling all over my skin, finding its way into the crevices of my body, inside, in other ways, making sure of itself, of me.

'Let me go,' I told my father, except I had no teeth, no learning. Looking up at him, he looking down at me, his face ruffling, cheeks sucking in and out, hair rippling; the clouds, the sun behind, high above, peeping through the trees, the same.

Let her go. Is that what he wanted? To let his baby daughter sink into the pool, to drown? Knowing, in that moment, what I had chosen; knowing, already, what I would one day do? Him, said to be, after all, someone who could read thoughts, and foretell the future? The beginning, the end.

I do not tell that he let me go. Do I remember that he let me go? Do I remember any of this, or is this a tale I pretend?

But… is this why I love the river? Is this why I swim under it, like the silver fish? Is this why I see all that passes through it, all that lives there? Or dies.

My father was the Master of Cynvael, as I have said.

Master of the House, the farm, the land around, the very spot chosen, to suit his inclinations ('best spot in the valley'… the valley, the commote, the cantref, Ardudwy), with the land shorn, then coaxed or pummelled into shape, accordingly.

The house was built by his own two hands, coupled with those of his brother, Owen—Owen's help later forgotten, so that it was, 'See, this beam…' pointing to the strut of oak straddling the hall hearth, holding the chimney up, the smoke and flames within—on a calm day, maybe. 'Hewn with my axe by me, alone, then carried on my shoulder to bring it here.'

I, too young, then, to cast my eye between wood and limb, to weigh the heft; too much younger, still, to mourn the cutting of the tree.

'Look at these stones, making our walls…' Some were thrown up by the earth, sent down by the river, given freely to him, each suited to its own place, space. There. 'There'.

But this…

'Feel this corner stone…' placing my hand on the largest riven rock, propping the house between river, earth and hill. 'Rolled down from the mountain, then carried across the water, in my arms.' Clenching his fists, turned upwards, the blue lines beneath his skin bruising, spreading, the stringy thews bulging. As if…!

He, seeing himself as strong as the giants fighting Arthur in the stories, seeing himself, too, like this stalwart stone, fixing all of this in its rightful place, holding it all together—the land, those that worked it; the house, those who kept it, the family, all of us, cosseted, cwtched within.

The family—his family—fashioned little by little, the wife, first, young, pert, and well-endowed, brought here from the Big House further west along the valley. For wasn't that endowment useful in making her new home a Bigger House, and better, should such consequences concern her?—which they did not, her being content as long as she had her spinning wheel, the loom, a garden, a hearth. Her harp. The Mistress of Cynvael, de jure.

His wife, *my mother*—but not then, not for a good while. First, the sons came, soon birthed. My brothers, as they were, though hardly known to me, existing in a separate time—a passed century, another monarch of different sex and dynasty (that Queen!)—a different world, you might say—with the years moving them forward until they were grown and departed. Me, glad of that, in time, or else they would, no doubt, try to command me, playing, as Gwydion did with Arianrhod, telling her what she must do. No surprise that she ran. Me, spared that by the slipped age.

Slipping on, until…

    … *me*. Me, with the story my mother gave me—how she, coming from visiting her old home, dismounted, to walk in the river, to cool her swollen ankles, and keep the heat at bay. How she was nearly here, when the pain struck, sending her crying, kneeling to the floor of the stream, where her waters broke forth—the breaking waters mingling with the water of the Cynvael. Her water, my water, river water, coming together, all the same. And then… me. 'You and me, the two of us, still entwined, struggling, then, against the flow, until your father's arms—your father, brought by my cries, or good old Apple running to him—lifting me, you, together, carrying us away!'

    She tells. A story I liked to hear, told on her knee, or where it happened. 'Here.' 'Here'. Or there… Sometimes, she tells, told, so that I could nod, and know the pull of the river. Never mind if it were another tale pretended—a good enough way to begin.

And then, yes, that man/saviour/father, with me, his only (living?) daughter. A daughter, loved, cherished, 'in the beginning' until… that baptism? The river reclaiming? Me, denying? Or… this…?

I saw my mother's belly swelling, felt it beneath me, as I suckled, felt, soon, the movement of another there. Felt her, in time, pushing me away, my father's arms, this time, lifting me (again), passing me to another. And soon I heard her screams—another story, birth-tale, all proper this time, but less charming. No river, no—replaced, instead, by the room next to mine, their room—no more than a bed, within four walls, with servant-women attending. It was just as it should be, if I had known what that was. Yet all I knew was screaming.

    My mother was dying, I thought, if I could think such horror. What else could make such cries—cries that sounded as if she were being torn apart? What could do that to her, but death coming?

And then another cry, a wail, not unlike my own, when I wanted food, or cwtching—the kind I made less, being older, replacing it with shouty lungs.

I shouted now. Someone would come, would see to me, the child, the star at the centre of this domestic heaven. But no. No-one came, and the cries lessened, hers and the other, and my shouts grew louder, and were still ignored, until my father appeared, carrying something scrappy and squally and bundled, and held it close to me.

'Look, you have a baby sister.'

Sister. Chwaer. Woman-kindred. Sweet sibling.

Lucky me...

'Let us give thanks to the Lord!'

I looked at her. She looked at me.

I hope—I like to think—I carried on shouting.

And now, his family was complete, his house—which he had made ('the best house', 'the best in the valley', 'the best in the' etc.)—complete. For she was the one, known at once, it seemed, the favoured, full-belonging, belonged, a perfect fit, the final piece in his plan.

So, yes, her, born precisely between its four walls, between the four posts of the marriage bed, in the master's/ mistress's room—the heart of the house, except for the hearth. Thus, the setting perfect, too. So there she was, tethered ever after to 'within', under its eaves, beneath its roof, breathing in *its* air, cast by its comings and goings, the words uttered and trapped inside. *His* words, more than any other, disgorged over her, read to her, taught to her— she, swallowing them down. Lap, lap.

His house, her house, his daughter, ever woven together. The true Mistress of Cynvael. Hers.

And yet, and yet...

Sometimes, I would hear that house speak to me, the parts of it from *its* beginning—*its* bones—as they were before they were taken from where they belonged, before he had forged them into what he wanted, shaped them to his needs. The trees, the stones. The wood, the mountain. Captured, then caught, here, around me, as I sat, silent, listening or watching.

The shifting of it in a storm, the cramping in the summer heat, the yearning of it, then, to return to what it once was. The oak keening. A straining, to break away from the pegs hammered into it, the chiselled joints. The wood spoke to me, then.

Or the flags whimpering, moisture seeping from them, where fingers of damp rose up from the river, inched along the ground, to sidle their way in. Wasn't that the river mourning its loss to me?

And the stones mouldering in the rain gathering on the back wall, wasn't that the lament of the mountains? While the mortar sifted with churchyard mould moaned with the ghosts of the ancients.

All wanting the house back, all working to make it so.

So it found me out, knowing *I* would pay attention, would acknowledge its longing. Me, not my sister. *Me.*

Her, shutting her eyes, her ears to such demands, wanting only the planed, polished side of it. The plastered walls, my mother's tapestries hung upon them, the carved finials, the neatly chamfered joints, the sealed stone; the dressed rooms—the parlour, the library, the study. The dais! Anything, everything that showed it closer to the great houses of the grand classes than a farmhouse wrought from and into a Welsh valley.

But yes, in truth, in fairness, no denying, the place was hers, more than mine, born, as she was, in that room, in that bed, her time spent within its walls far longer than my days spent roaming outside, her inclination keeping her there; him, keeping her there, if he were there himself, until…

And yes, back to that room again, beside the bed, sitting beside it those hours, days, weeks, when he lay in it, breathing his last… and beyond.

'Come,' I said to her.

'Come away.'

'Come,' my mother said to her. My mother, who carried on in her garden, at her wheel, the hearth. 'Enough.'

'Come,' my brothers said to her, waiting to claim their inheritance, based on law, rather than due.

But no, she was not ready. Not then. Words not spoken, then.

Fair enough, maybe. It all harder for her, all that had happened, whatever that was, as best we could tell.

The best I do to tell, here.

For…

My father was the Magician of Cynvael. The conjuror, the dewin. (Was, is. Some say he never died. We say yes, no, depending. Decided on whom we are talking to, reading in their eyes what they want to know. Saying 'yes' to the believers, both of heaven and magic, the kind who seek resurrection for themselves, through God or charm.)

'You'll not find pieces of paper to prove it,' is what history will say, history liking some such, lines of black ink dotted and dashed onto parchment. Blotted. Put safely away into tight drawers in vaulted buildings, flattened or scrolled. No, there are none of that kind, nor entry into the fat book of the church, in the fine hand of the Rector of St Twrog's, our neighbouring parish. You might think the good Rector would know. True, he was not Edmund Prys, 'Tŷ-du', Archdeacon, neighbour, friend of my father's, 'friend'/rival, fellow claimant for this or that crown—the Reverend Prys having himself most definitely died a few years before (or did he?—history confusing that, too). But, still, whoever. And no, there are no thicker, deeper letters, chiselled out of stone, put at the head of a grave, because there is no grave. Something else the good Rector might explain. And no plaque on the farm-house wall, like the maybe/son/nephew/same one, one-in-the-same, or nothing to do with.

(But 'was' or 'is', while he was alive.)

… my father was the Magician of Cynvael, pulling a silver penny from behind your ear, picking the right card from a pack, disappearing in a cloud of smoke, a shroud of mist, emerging from the same.

I, you, me, we watching, another trickster memory of a trick.

Tucked behind a bush, crouched beneath a rock, pushing through the knees of the villagers, as they huddle closer, I watch as they watch, their breath caught between their lips, as the mist grows thicker above the stream. I hear their 'ohs' and 'ahs' as the fog shreds and wavers, giving way to a giant shaping before their eyes. 'A giant,' they say. 'My father,' I think, watched, before, in our parlour, donning robe upon robe, becoming broader; pulling on high-heeled boots, to grow taller. Oh, those robes! Patterned with talismans, the wide hems shamming his height. The whip he carried at his belt, a handle of bone, the skin of an eel (an eel – a poor man's caduceus!) And the hat he wore to top it off—a high-crowned sheepskin, with a plume of pigeon feathers. Such a show! Whilst his revelation was no more than the knowledge of the brightest sun burning off the morning mist of the slow autumn water.

This is how a giant is made, how magic is made of the 'now you see me, now you don't' kind.

And now you see me, them, the same simple folk gathered round (but not too close, the whip drawing his circle of awe), further down the cwm, further into the trees—how they love this—as he charms the birds down from the trees. Their mouths as open as the birds, chirruping as excitedly as their feathered friends, at the wonder of it all. Not knowing what I know, that the fluttering creatures are just-hatched chicks, stolen from their mothers' nests and stored in cages in the secret corners of our barn, crumb-fed, hand-fed, by him, day after day.

Crumbs hidden now, beneath his spacious sleeve, his finger-tips thumb-rubbed, tempting, calling, mimicking their songs. Breath held, then released, in aaaws and gasps, folk easily pleased, birds easily pleased, tame, now, all of them.

There is more, of course. Bigger than these little shows, these sleights of hand, these legerdemain, hoodwinks of eye and tiny minds. Happenings talked about for years to come, stories spread, hand to mouth, along the valley, into the villages, further into the towns. Across the borders, even, towards the English Court. Stories told by the old stock, generations fed by what they like to hear.

Some were given names, 'titles', written on parchment, then in books, safe-keeping for all time, no argument. Printed, passed from hand to hand, 'mouth' being too old-fashioned then.

'The Magician of Cynvael foils Two Witches'—the favourite tale, most told, dispersed by those he 'aided'—travellers who came to him from the Betws-y-Coed inn, where their pride and purses had been dented by its captivating sister-owners.

'My door was locked!'

'My window was fastened!'

'There were no other guests—only the two women inn-keepers were there!'

He went himself, dressed in his full military regalia, sword in hand—or so he told—and came back, triumphant.

'Witches...' he proclaimed.

'... turning themselves into cats, sneaking in and stealing that way.'

'They won't be doing it again.' Ho, ho, ho—him, laughing, then; Lizzie sitting at his feet, laughing, too, hee,

hee, hee. While I wanted to scream, 'If I hear this tale again!' Scream… and spew…

Shall I tell you the tale anew? I, who was there when he returned, whip in hand, red strands on its tip, a grin spread from ear to ear. I, who listened to his words of those cats caught and paws/hands sliced with his sword, pronounced in triumph to the ones the 'hags' had tricked.

A whip is better than a sword, I try to believe. A girl's back more hidden than a hand, I know.

Shall I tell you something other? How the two were not 'hags' at all—were no more than two women, keeping an inn to get by? True, maybe, they added a little water to each jug of ale, and upped its price to the cut of cloth. But what canny innkeeper won't do the same? Yet they were women, fleecing men. And they were women of 'prepossessing appearance', who paid no attention to the overtures of the male. For they were not even 'sisters'— something my father, for all his 'observation', did not spy. Not seeing the way they looked at each other, a touch as they passed. Not wanting to see…

And shall I say his next take on the tale? How he couldn't let it/them go? Telling this story of foiling them again, walking backwards when they wished to curse. Of reaching the church and laying a spell, so they would never witch again.

Of bandits entranced by horns sprung from a table. Or was that what rival Prys did to him?—a rumour quickly quashed! Of the Devil and weed. Of fiends summoned at the Fall, and farmers punished. Of, of, of. Such magic wrought by the Magician of Cynvael, worker of miracles. Such magic as had never been seen!

Something else I know—my father says he brought the magic here, but it has always been here, or since times remembered in the stories. There is a far older magic in this place, a truer kind, where a witch lives in the heart of the wood, a friend to its creatures, gathering its offerings into healing balms. Where stone heads take court, from those who worship them, an ancient cult. Where the trees themselves dispense their wisdom, as far and wide as their roots will spread.

All these filling the older tales, whispered, along with where the giants live, fighting Arthur's knights, and the stories of those others that fill my dreams. The flower-maiden, the moon goddess, the vengeful lover/warrior—all played and pulled like puppets, according to *his* game.

Gwydion. The true magician.

I see *him*, too, in my dreams—the ones that visit me when I sleep in the wood, where he, too, liked to roam. Gwy-di-on. Hearing his name whispered by the trees, that he was lord of, amongst all his other subjects. Hearing his laugh, in the rustle of the branches. 'Here,' he says to me. And there he is, sitting high in their arms, or low in the cleft of a hollow trunk, or flying between them; making them grow or wither, spread or gather. Herding them, sometimes, as if they are beasts. In my dreams, watching *his* magic. No coins behind the ears or marked cards for him, as he takes one being, casts his spell and lo! it is something quite changed, a different form altogether! Watching the swine become horses, the girl become an owl, the girl he made out of flowers. Coming across him, as he searched for Lleu, his nephew, speared by Gronw, and turned into an eagle. Maggots lie on the ground, fallen from the topmost branches, feeding on gobs of flesh shaken down. Lleu, corrupted, the king of the birds corrupted, until Gwydion's englyn, his song.

Awake, I see there is no eagle. It is, instead, a buzzard, pulling at a pigeon, clamped in its claws.

Awake, I stand where he stood, here, at the edge of my river. 'Here.' He says again. And there he is, behind me, in front of me, above me. Everywhere, reminding me it is not *my* river, it is no-one's river, or wood, or mountain, if it is not his, and whether it is his is still a 'maybe'.

What might he do to me, I wonder, if he should so choose? Change me, as he did Blodeuwedd? But is it so bad to be an owl, I ask? Frisking through the boughs, together with the fractured moonbeams. The moon—another magicking—Arianrhod, his sister, from an earlier part of the story—his doing, still—it is always *his* doing. Present time, past time, forever, time gone.

I shake my head, I rub my eyes, I wake, if I am asleep. Like one of his spells, *he* is gone. For now. Gwy-di-on, son of Dôn. The Magician of all the magicians, of all the stories…

… that my fool of a father thought he could mirror! More than that—as if he were him, come back again! Choosing this place, where the river joins the mountains to the sea, with us and the wood in between, beginning, ending, taking-your-pick between once-upon-a-time and Amen, to follow in his footsteps. Calling up his name, dabbling his spells, in poor mimicry. Until…

… the ultimate incantation. Another reawakening, another restoration. Somewhere, anywhere. No need for certificates, nor gravestones, nor even burial in the ground. No need for any of those. Just a few words spun, as deft as a spell. Saving the best trick till last.

My sister and I helped/help the tales along, now, using them in a magic-show of our own. Using them to mask doings of our own, to stop questions before they are asked. We made a magic-show of it, then, making up the last story of the Magician of Cynvael, choosing our words, Lizzie, the wordy one, sculpting them aright. *No* this. *No* that. Yes, that will do. Let this be the story that's told. Let this be the story, like that other, that's handed down in books, Lizzie being good at books and their writing. People like stories of magic folk in lakes, of hands rising from them, of magic still spelled at the end of such a life—another mirroring of the old, another King, Arthur. (Yes, let it be something like that.) Only here the truth is told. Maybe.

My father was the preacher of Cynvael, stealing the role from the Reverend Prys (while the good Reverend still lived), using his enchanter's tricks and his crowd-pleasing performances. Poor Reverend, Rector, Archdeacon Edmund, trapped behind his lectern, in his cold-boned church. My father, instead, standing on the tower of stone in the middle of the stream, calling it his Pulpit, reciting from the Holy Book. 'Holy Father, Lord, Our Father.'

(*Your* father, half the time, meaning. His words, chosen for praising the Father of man, so often praising the father of two little girls. Us. Him.

(Our Father/father did this, Our Father/father did that. Our father ruled the world, our world, the lord of the manor. There were many rooms there.

(Whatever.)

So he stood on his pulpit—a slanted, slatted stack, raised from the rushing stream, or fallen down it, and crammed to rest. And he clothed himself in black, a vicar's cassock, this time, plain and flowing, to paint the difference; the Bible in his hands. Perching there, in boots flat and wide, their soles scored, to make their clench stronger, their soles dabbed with pitch to make them stick, so that he stood firm, against the slime of the water-weed, the ceaseless spray of the torrent, the wind funnelling through the valley's steep sides—the want of the needy crowd. They, clung together, perched as best they could on the lower, flatter stones, their faces uplifted, shining… feigning. Yes. Feigning.

River.

'Thank you, Cynvael!' The words that gush from his mouth, spilling into your waters below, getting lost there in the stirring, the churning, the frothing. I watch them go, imagining God broken into G O D, each letter spiralling down, down, leaping and dancing along the falls. Seeing the L O R D sink to the bottom, and settle into the sediment, to be eaten by the sucking fishes, while J E S U S floats apart and bobs away, all the way to the sea. Goodbye,

Jesus, goodbye, all.

Still on and on, my father goes, his words go, because he doesn't know that his flock of worshippers can't hear, hearing only the river. And none of them to tell him different.

And Lizzie, when she was old enough to join the faithful band, would say, 'Thank you, Father, such a wonderful sermon,' while I sniggered in the corner.

Once, some time after my baptism, he took me up there with him, still hopeful of me then, no Lizzie to compare with, no alien notions uttered yet on my part, wanting to show me off to the crowd. His baptised babe in arms—his arms, holding me tight, until something stuttered in them, as we climbed. A muscle? A sinew? A nerve trapped between two bones? The tiniest cramping. His legs, beneath me, still in the water… the slightest tremor… until up, little by little, we began to climb.

I like to think I wriggled then, to make it harder, to make us fall. He would topple, I would tumble with him, splash into the water. What a fool he would look, floundering like a beached trout, flailing around for his drowning daughter. Where had his God gone, now? (As if I could devise such a plan at such a young age, as if I could butt my elbow against his chest on purpose, and push my knee against the rock, wave my foot in the air.)

But, no, he didn't fall. Some will held him together, tightening his sinews, tautening his nerves—freeing the one caught between his bones… pushed him up the last stretch, so that he was there, on the top again, with me still in his arms, when all the people gathered cheered.

And maybe I did, or didn't think or do such mischief. Because… how could I remember? How can I remember, what is or isn't true—that, or anything else—at such a young age? And maybe I am foolish—no, I am almost certainly foolish, wrong, in truth—to believe that all his words were lost to the river, that the river stole them away. For, otherwise, why would the sheep keep on flocking, in spite of their soakings from the spray, why would Lizzie swear to the power of his speech, why would the Reverend Prys stand lonely in his church, every time my father preached? And why would legend have it, thus, down through all the years?

So I must allow that G O D came out of his mouth, each letter clear as the throstle's first note in Spring, bellowed loud as Tŷ Graig's black bull. It joined together across the water, the word coming whole again, as it reached the bank, and the harking ears. It joined with the LORD JESUS and ALMIGHTY and the coming of the KINGDOM and life everlasting, if you follow OUR FATHER's will. HIS will. Him.

Words rising above the river, they must be, words transfixing his audience. WORDS, Words, words. WORDS, telling the flock how it should live, behave in the eyes of the Lord, his *eyes*, in particular, here, in *his* valley, to make life here the best it could, should be, according to him. Do this, that, the other. Don't do this, that, the other. And you will all go to Heaven, happily ever after. A reward, if the Cynvael isn't heaven enough for you…

There were other words, too, at other times. A different kind of wording, the Lord and his kind not showing themselves so much amongst them. Softer sounds, singing together, telling tales of animals, the fox, the deer, the eagle. Poems, he called them, capturing the creatures from the wild, trapping them in metre and verse, as if such a thing could happen. As if the slink of the vixen, as she moves through the long grass could be tethered, as if he could recognise its ripple! As if the stare of the hare's eye could be levelled, in a 'welcome to fertile country.'

Rhymes to be told around the hearth, or to gatherings in halls, among others doing the same, each trying to outdo each other—yes, poor Prys there again. My father claiming the crown for himself, another hand-me-down from Gwydion, the master-bard, the chief story-teller, the word-wizard.

I sit on the mountain, behind the crags, watching the hare below. What I feel far outweighs the charm of his rhymes, my heart lifted, soaring, my pulse quickened. Why should he—or any of them—bother?

Words… words of meddling kind—the commands and commandments, the spells and the enchantments, holy or melody. Born in his head, simpered or spat through his lips, sent forth to weave their way over, around, through us, tangling in their thrall, like knitting bewitched near a field. Warping. My mother's spinning pulled away from her wheel and made flesh! Binding our feet here, wrapping our thoughts up tight, stifling our ears and eyes. Done from our earliest years—us and all who came near to him.
'Pull the thread,' I told myself. 'Loosen the tie, undo the knots.'
'Pull the thread,' I tell myself. 'Sort out the weft and woof, go back to the beginning.'
His, ours. The river's. The valley's. The wood's. The story's. Cynvael's. This.

So… to rewind the threads, again—my father was the Master, Magician, Preacher, poet of Cynvael. Was, in fact, many other guises, too, more of which later, as we go along. A shape-shifter, by profession, by sleight of hand, by connivance—pure and simple, switching with the time, the place, the audience, the need. We, needing to look beneath, to find the constant, as best we can. As follows, as best we can.

My father was born in 1568. That was told by my grandfather, his father, Dafydd Llwyd ap Howel ap Rhys, is told by my mother, and is proven, according to a piece of paper, existing, this time—strange, in fact, that the older should endure, while the newer… what? Born, therefore, in the time of the Old Queen, lived to see her die, on through the time of the new King, then on into the next reign, for… how long? Ah, that is the question. My father died in 1620, 1628, or 1629 or 1630. Hard to say for sure, without that other certificate, or that writing in the book, on the stone. Hard to say, therefore, if he died, at all, with no will written, no probate granted—which is why the doubt exists—what with no reason for dying given, beyond another Magician's tale, where he lay in his bed, lingering, and… Which, in truth, we spun.

His names shifted, too. But then, it was the same for all of us in those times, between the two languages, between friends, foes and kin; the properties' blessing. So he was Hu, Huw, Hugh, Lloyd, Llwyd. Huw Cynfal, Huw Llwyd o Gynfal, Cunuel, Huw Cynvael—him, favouring 'Cynvael' most, thinking it sounded courtly, suited to England, as well as Cymru. Cynfal-fawr, Cynvael Fawr. Lloyd Hughes. Hu the Mighty, named after the strongman hero—how he liked that one, when heard it whispered by the farm-folk! Morgan Llwyd, even, on occasion—a generation slipped and muddled. (He, of the blue plaque. My uncle or nephew… or my brother—which? How could he be born here, if not my brother? A chance visit by his mother, so that his birth here was chance? Yet, if my brother, how was *he* not the chosen one? Or… how could two such skilled learneds both dwell here? Is it no more than a muddle of records muddling, or a story unexplained? But I will let that one go, leave it for another. It is not mine to tell.)

My father… Father. *Our* father, not in heaven, but here. Father of daughters, his second brood, come late.

Yes, that is another of his nomenclature, his 'occupations'—the least that mattered, the most important, the reason for it all, all that happens here. This one mine, my sister's, and… The two (?) of us. Us, past the birthing, starting to grow, growing.

Another beginning. Another scritching of the fibres to

turn it into a yarn. Hark. Listen. Hear it. Not the river, now. Us.

My name is Mared. Maaah-red. Roll that around your tongue, too. Call it—a good name for calling, for my mother to call, from the house door, whenever she could not find me, whenever I was off wandering in the wood, by the river, up, even, as far as the mountain, as if the name could reach me, there. Called by my mother, also, as in 'named' by her. Strange, that he should have allowed it, but, yes, he did, somehow. A nod to *her* mother, Margaret—it being a form of that, but not the same. A Welsh name, meaning a pearl—something precious, something bright, found under the water. Her saying how, after all the fuss and fury of the birth had quieted, she had found the shell clasped to the hem of her cloak, its silver treasure still within. A daughter, at last, given to her, precious, indeed. A gift of nature, a natural prize.

My sister is Lizzie, Elizabeth, named after the old Queen, the virgin Queen (the 'virgin' bit being much favoured, by men, we understand), dead before we were born, but still remembered, revered, by him, at least—he, having soldiered for her; more, it is sometimes rumoured; she was fond of spies and their spying, among many other interests, among learning in reading, writing, mathematics, languages from foreign shores; this, that, the other— cutting people's heads off…

E-liz-a-beth. An English name, long, with several sounds. No wonder we shrunk it down.

Strange, it was, as if we were shaped already by our parents, by our names, though shapes shift, we learned very quickly as we grew. Nothing is as fixed as you think it may be.

Still, he helped it from the start. He, our father. 'He' in this story is usually our father, when he is not God, or the Devil—(who are, in fact, sometimes, all one in the same). He forged the differences, tarred the brushes, pasted the different labels, came between us. As if, at that very first moment, he looked down on Elizabeth, as he had once looked down on me, and known *she* was the one, having given up on me already.

Soon, I saw devotions from my cot never witnessed before. Watched, as he whispered over the cradle's edge, passing secrets to his gurgling bab. Saw him slipping a crystal under her pillow, to keep against the evil eye; hang a bag with the Gospel writ in it, from the carved spindles of her bed. Wrought a star into its wooden sides, a five-pointed pattern, to keep-safe and seep power.

All these rituals he performed that he had never done for me. Though how would I know? But then, how would I know any of this? Or ken his meaning when he told all who visited, who valued such matters, 'She is the seventh child, of me, the seventh son of a seventh son. We are the chosen ones.' He, of course, was the unadulterated male, blessed with the fullest array of powers, proof of his superiority, if any needed. But Lizzie was special… enough… too.

And they would nod, and oh and ahhh, and gaze in wonder, never using their heads to question the choice, the reckoning, happy to swallow down this seventh child, no seventh son being available, the daughter sufficient, if that were the case.

Whereas I…

… starting with him, counting them off on my fingers, as soon as I was old enough to put two known, and four mentioned together.

'Where is the other? There is uncle Owen for sure. There are the four whose names float in and out, when suits, long gone from the valley. But never seven.'

'Perhaps he died, in birth, or childhood and Father

doesn't like to talk of it. Or perhaps he doesn't even remember him. It would still count as seven, wouldn't it? If he were the seventh born, he is the seventh son.' She with her numbers, playing such games.

'And he has eaten the flesh of the eagle, hasn't he? We have heard the tale…'

Yes, we had heard it, as he told it to folk gathered round—how he had shot the bird on Eryri, eying his prey so sharp, even as it flew, sending his arrow so swift after, a perfect shot through its heart. How he saw to the fallen creature, himself, there on the slope where it had fallen, plucking its feathers from it, saving them for his charmer's dress. Peeling the skin from it, slicing the flesh from the bone, eating it raw from the tip of his knife. Cruel, to kill that magnificent bird—a sacred bird, no less. All done for the sake of the future generations… for Lizzie, it would be.

Told to us, too, time and time again, till I, fed up of it, asked 'What did it taste like, this eagle?'

'Chicken,' he replied, straight.

As if… as if the king of the skies could bear the same meat as the pathetic, clucking hens, who pester our doorstep, who give us no more than a scrag of flesh between them/us.

And then, later, with his own brood, no seven children, either.

'Where are the others?' I said to Lizzie, counting us off on my fingers, putting three and two together.

'Huw, Tom, Gareth, me, you. Five, that comes to.' Naming our big brothers, dragging them back into our existence, from whatever lives they were living elsewhere.

'More lost babies,' she replied, quick as anything. 'Like happened before, because it happens all the time, Mam not wanting to talk about it, for the hurt.' She had picked up the talk of the maids, perhaps, or read it from a book, Lizzie having already read so many books by then. Or from my father—had he explained it to her, spelling out her inheritance, wanting her to take on the role, from the start?

Lost babies, or children unaccounted. Yes, happened, happens all the time. Or… the whispers we heard in the night, the cries, or the cold breath that passed through our room, or… somewhere out there, a different 'other world' from my brothers, not so far, but still unseen. Just out of reach, or just down below the water, lost.

Perhaps. Whichever, whatever, somehow, Elizabeth/Lizzie was the seventh child of a seventh son.

'And have *you* eaten the flesh of an eagle, because you have to, don't you? And he said he'd brought it to you. What did it taste like?'

'I did not!' she told me, her nose curling. 'Hen,' she whispered, 'it's what he gave me, fresh caught and killed that morning, broiled, so still pale, and told me to pretend.'

I laughed—that he had spared her that, for, otherwise, as I have said, her birthright and privilege began straight away—her destiny mapped out in those signs and symbols on her crib, crafted soon as she/we grew, into words, words, words—inside, now, not the words sprayed onto others across rivers—those words from his mouth flooding over her/me—me, caught in the deluge, unable to avoid them, in my early years. His words of learning, teaching, spoken, that pedant's cap nodding along with him. Yes, yes, yes.

Spoken, then read. Yes, that, too. Trapped words unleashed.

Because, of course, that was something else my father possessed—he, the preacher, the teacher, the learned man had a library, the foremost in Wales, he declared— confirmed since by others, disputed by those who liked to claim the same for themselves—the reverend Prys/Pryse/ Price again. Poor Reverend Prys, so often outdone by his rivalrous friend.

I hated that room from the first. It was another place I was carried to, babe in arms, as if he wanted to enthral me in its charms, steep me in its perfume. Except I did not see it that way, with the covers still stinking from the cows they had come from, the binding from the detritus of dead horse—the smell niggling up my nose; the ink smarting my eyes, eyes caught between widening on account of the dimness, and shutting to keep out that hurt. Because, yes, the drapes were drawn close to keep the sunlight at bay, for fear of fading the precious words.

Words from another's head, not his own. Row after row of titles read out to me, as if they were meant to be a lullaby, when all they did was screch against my ears. 'Brytannicae Rei…'; '…Descriptionis Fragmentum.'

And then one volume would be edged from its place, one-handed, me balanced beside; it, placed on the desk, gently opened, whatever it offered given to me, as if I would drink it like my mother's milk, or the water of the river. The fodder that could be found there! Dust, drone, blah, blah. Dull. Drear. I stretched my neck towards the one sliver of light, where the curtains failed to meet. I sent my arms after, and pushed with my knees. I had learnt greater command of my limbs by then. I had learnt, too, how to use my lungs, when I wanted, or didn't want, something. I opened them wide, my mouth matching. Tears splashed down towards the precious pages. And he knew, that with screeching like this, puking could follow. Oh, his horror, as he imagined milky puke dissolving the words, the coloured illustrations, the paper itself. Gone! Oh, his face, as he/we beat a hasty retreat!

Soon, it didn't matter. He had Lizzie in my stead. Lizzie, who would cwtch in his arms, reach up with her tiny fingers for his words, catching them from the start, catching them, swallowing them all, taking them as gospel, the gospel as gospel, together with all the other bound, paginated 'wisdom' found there. In the beginning was the word, most definitely for Lizzie. In the beginning, yes, in his arms, then taken on his knee, the book in his hands, keeping her tight. And, as she went on, she was given her own place to sit, a chair in the corner, where she spent hour after hour of her days, finger following the twists and turns of each letter, of each page, of each book, lips mouthing, eyes beaming. Happy.

Until… I would appear, peeping around the door, making faces at her, uttering words of my own.

'Lizzie. Lizzie. Lizabeth. Bethie! What are you doing, Lizzie? Oooo, whooo. Na, na.'

'Na, na…Ow!' A hand on my shoulder, my father, picking me up by the scruff of my neck, carrying me inside, Lizzie smirking all the while. Time for our lessons, 'Lesson time!' for yes, we must be taught, by him, after the break of fast, before the strike of noon, if he were at home, not gone elsewhere, if he had nothing more pressing to do—we, his daughters, being so, so lucky that he would do this for us, he told us, being girls. For girls were seldom allowed such a blessing, which is what 'learning' was. A blessing, therefore, that he taught us; a blessing, that he had been… a soldier.

Yes, my father was the 'general' of Cynvael, another manifestation, this one from his youth, held onto into age.

Held in the way his body holds itself erect, his legs march in straight lines, he shaves his hair and beard trim and tight, he keeps his muscles taut. Held in the way his words snap when he wants something done, ordering my mother, Lizzie, me; my brothers, even, when they are come back, no matter they are grown men, no matter they have been soldiers, themselves. Seen, also, in the way he kills— for he has killed men, it is what soldiers do, learning fighting skills. Here, it is animals he kills, despatching them with a swift thrust, a lean slice, no hesitation there.

All this disregarding how many years have gone, for he was a soldier serving under the old Queen, before the changeling king, singing her praises and her ways, even after all these years. 'How learned she was, how much attention she paid to her studies, from a young age!' And it would be the same for us, never minding that we did not have the best minds in the land, its greatest thinkers, having, instead, my father. Just as good, according, of course, to him. And Lizzie.

For 'soldiering' meant travelling to distant lands,

broadening the mind, viewing new ways and ideas, all waiting inside his head, to drone through his lips, into our ears, our heads. 'Hooray!'

'You pick up this and that in foreign parts,' he told us, once. He had told us many times before.

But this time, I was at an age to think 'pox', sniggering to myself, while Lizzie pictured trinkets, mementos, like the Flemish lace draped over the sofa, or the silver belt buckle, come from Ottoman lands, that Father wore, that she coveted for herself.

'Tongues,' he said.

Tongues, cut out of enemies, I thought. I knew such abominations happened—overheard conversations, in his own house, being a source of knowledge my father was ignorant of. I knew how the 'noble victors' behaved after the battle. I pictured it—a knife drawn quick, slicing through the pink flesh, wrapped in a kerchief, pocketed and later dried. A different version of Lizzie's 'mementos', ferreted back here, in the weed pouch, perhaps, or wrapped in a rug. Here, somewhere? I had ferreted, myself, by then, into all the nooks and crannies of the place. And oh, the traps I had found... but no tongues, I think, unless they were beyond knowing, time suck-sapping them out, seeping their colour—brown, withered, a prune, or fig, perhaps, or mistaken for the sole of a soldier's boot, buried in mud and blood, shrunk by that drying... and that 'time'.

'No,' he said, 'not that.' He had this way of divining, looking at me, his head to the side, seeing behind my eyes. I worked to keep my head lowered in his company, but did not always succeed.

'Words, the languages other nations speak. Words, here, phrases, there, whole understanding with some.'

'Not that,' mimicked Lizzie. 'The speech of distant lands.'

Languages. First and foremost, he wanted us to speak both Welsh and English. We would speak Welsh in front of certain people—our neighbours in the cwm of the Afon

Cynfal—English for others—visitors from away, visiting the valley of the River Cynvael. Another chop-and-change, following him, to be both Welsh and English, to suit the times. And, later, for us, his daughters, it would suit our marriage prospects, widening the field. Sometimes, I did not know who I was…

And for Lizzie, there was more, wanting *her* to learn other tongues, too. 'Her Majesty spoke several languages, including Welsh,' he was fond of saying. 'Our Lizzie will be the same.' Not me, he said. I did not have the 'aptitude.' 'Good,' I told my sister. 'It is a waste of time,' yet had this strange dip in the stomach, a nag in my mind.

So yes, my father was a soldier, the way he could say hello in Spanish, and Hollandish, and ask 'How are you?' in French, should you want to possess such useful knowledge—which Lizzie did, and soon could do the same, together with so much other learning.

For 'read to' was turned to reading, turning to writing, in double-quick time.

The mouthed words, the words followed along the page with her finger, then snatched and caught in her head, turned to line and curve on parchment, slowly, at first, but then, so soon, more quickly. Scrawls and squiggles, a single word, changed into neat phrases, sentences, paragraphs. HIS words—that is what it came to, in time. His words, copied down by her—the words that sprang from him, as he stood on that rock, the poems, his teachings. The words brought back from his journeys. Gifts, he called them, traveller's tales, stories in which he was the hero. The stories of his exploits, as magician, soldier, everything, with Lizzie sitting at his feet, doe-eyed, hanging on to every word, swallowing them all, ready to gather them together, with the reams he had written beforehand, preparing.

Up to—'A book, we shall make a book of them, Father, so that they can be shared far and wide, so that the word can be spread.'

'A book of your own, to house between all the other books you own.'

And so it was, is, right to the end and beyond. There she was, is, frantically writing at his bedside, Lizzie, the keeper of the story.

And so, yes, this was how Lizzie would spend her days, from their earliest, in that library, that I hated and she loved. And this was how it would be when we were old enough to step outside and roam—

'It's a beautiful day, Lizzie. Take your head out of that book. Come and run through the wood!'

Come and swim in the pools of the river.

Come and climb up the mountains, see the world from there.

'The world is here,' she would say, lifting whatever book she was reading. 'A far wider world than our meagre hills and dales.'

'But the sun is out there, the sky, the earth. Air, to breathe. What more do we need?'

'Plenty,' she would reply, and she would begin reading, just as he had done, thinking to entice me to her side, with the power of these wondrous words. But I didn't need the strength of my lungs or the retch of my stomach to escape, any more. My legs took me quickly enough, back through the house, back outside, across the river, into the wood, again. Where, yes, I could breathe.

Foolish Lizzie, her skin pale, like the stalks of the plants trapped under a stone, her growth stunted, like saplings struggling for light in the deepest part of the wood; her eyes narrow and dim, grown too used to candle light and narrow focus. And there I was, with my own brown face, my solid limbs, my wide, bright eyes, taking in everything around them, drinking in the world, that way.

And I would tell her this, when bile was spitting back and forth between us, mocking the look of her. But she would laugh, and point to her head, and say, 'But I have far more in here!'

So I would laugh louder, and twirl my fulsome body in front of her, yet in 'here', there would be a niggle, a creeping of doubt and annoyance. And I would flounce off outside, to fling my arms wide, in welcome to the earth and the sky, to tell myself how much more they taught me.

Yes.

River birthed me, wood raised me.

That is how I see it.

My mother… my mother. My mother, who came from legend, too. From further south and west, whence Gwydion came, where Blodeuwedd and Gronw played. My mother sitting at her harp, my mother spinning at her wheel, my mother bent over her plants. This was/is my mother's world, her on the inside, smiling out at me, at Lizzie, at all of us, as if the notes of her music, the fluff from her yarn, the aroma of her blossoms mingled together and wrapped themselves around her, and us apart. Always near, always far, loving but distant. Fair enough, I came to think, as I grew older. Fair enough, to work out a way to survive his ways, him.

Him… him, the Manifest of many, all these different men muddled together, yet I could not find 'father' in there—not the father I wanted, for all there were so many possibilities, because I was unable to make sense of who he really was. Lizzie, of course, had no trouble finding him— found him by being like him, by having so much in common. Who inherited his skills? Who was his rightful/ chosen 'heir'? Who followed in his footsteps? Plain to see— Lizzie.

Something else plain to see—that he had no time to be 'father' if you did not have the want, need to fit in with him, if you did not want to play at being 'daughter'.

So…

'The wood.'

The Cynvael wood.

'The water feeds the soil, the seed grows in the soil. Over time, an age of time…' Another of my father's lessons, told to us, of how the wood the other side of the river was formed.

But let *me* tell you about the wood, and what lives within. Let me tell you in my own way. Let me look back into the past, and see myself as the girl I was, and how I lived back then, where I went, when Lizzie shrugged me, when Mother was lost in her woven dreams, when my father bristled his brows and turned away.

Cross the river, at the lower ford, much where you were born, trip, trapping across the stones. Ignore the willow! Yes, no matter how you favour it, loving it for its closeness to the stream, how it drinks from it, as you did; for its cleaving to the moon. Envying how it bends with the current, unlike your own stubbornness; savouring inspiration from its wavering wands.

No! Slip, instead, between the clefted rock, shed by the mountain, and burrow your way up, in. Beetle-spread, over or under the fallen trunks, moss-fleeced, fern and fungus pitted, scattering misplaced fairy-hats along the way. Your hand smoothing the fur as you go, wanting to pause, to explore the world beneath it, on the bark of the sycamore, of the beech, of the… but, no—you will wait for the oak for that; the oak offers so much more. The Oak, the king of the trees (queen, Mother—whichever you favour), of the valley, the true ruler of Cynvael, if you look at it another way, the right way.

So, greet the rowan, the alder, the elder and ash, as they crowd upon you, and take their greetings in return—a bow from their slender boughs—but wait for the Oak for more, only… they do not want you to pass, wanting you to stop a while, and talk to them instead. And they stretch out their arms, hoping to catch you, or nudge up their roots, yearning to trip you.

'Be careful, now; be very careful.' It being unlucky to break off the branch of an ash tree. And if it snags you, do not remain too long in its company, it being a spirit-trapped tree (and who knows who or what lies within?). Yet… yet… if you want to know secrets… and a branch, freely given, has certain powers…

Still, not as many as the Oak, none has as many powers as the Oak. So on, on you go. On, on, into the heart of the wood, to where it stands, the parent tree—for them, for me.

In the beginning, when you are smallest, you stand at the bottom, arms stretched round, as far as they will go, neck cricked up, as far as it will go. You are glad to see it, glad to have something to embrace. To *feel*. *This* is where you can stop a while, your eyes, your fingers, seeking that miniature world. A ridge of mountains, an abyss, a forest, a stream, where the sap flows through—all there. A labyrinth knotting the trunk. Your eyes—what you see—tree, wood, bark, yes, but *this*, to begin. Colour. Colours not taught, tree-bound, green, brown. There is white, here; white, on a tree. Bird-spattered? No! Fairy tricks? No! You have seen this on stones, too, where the Tylwyth won't go. White, merging to dried-leaf sage. 'Lichen,' he said, once—you, not wanting the name, him proud of it, newly-found. 'From the Latin, the Greek. A plant. It is said to remedy hydrophobia, when reduced to a powder, if…'

No, not this. *This*, a shade, a hue, nothing else. Daubed, to garland the tree. Woven together by tendrils of shadows, up from the crevices below. Black. And gold, the golden cloak of the oak. Gold—not dullard brown!

You move, from eyes to fingers, craving the texture. 'Lichen, a plant.' Yes, in this, perhaps he is right—what you brush your hands through. Bristling, from bark. Sheep-shorn. Not like the moss, the moss lower down, the moss facing the north, a huntsman's velvet jacket. Up and down your hands go, your palms gently grazed, your hands idling through the shrunken forest, or dried-out pondweed on water's brow. Then, that moss—soft, silken fur, cropped, or springy, or curled, bearded, according to breed.

Time to burrow, to find the world within. Fingertips small enough, to ferret between the furrows ploughed through its rind. To startle the wood-beetles boring deep; to squelch the grubs, lying in wait. Uhh! Scuffing the roots of the ferns, sprouting forth, thwarted by the suckered paws of the ivy, ants tickling, as you go. Them, avoiding, you, avoiding, the glue of spiders' webs. But no good, caught between your nails, them, catching the insects—honeydew and sap-drunk; them, caught by the cobweb beetle, on and on and on, one into the other. Squelching, again, against the fungus, like dead, rotten flesh, its stems mapping out, sinking in, in. Deeper, deeper, holed, now. Homes for birds, bats—so many bats!—leave well alone, feel, no more.

Back away, for you, for them. But come again. 'Soon.'

Older, you climb, the fissured bark giving you finger-holds, fingers stronger, around the pliant branches, given to you, you are sure, wanting your ascent. You can reach trunks you can hug fully, holding their girth close, an unyielding body. Then up, up, the boughs get smaller and smaller, until you reach those that cannot bear your weight—the top for you, but not for it. Above, there is still so much of its being, those wisps of wood, twig, carrying on into the sky, their leaves dancing against the blue, grey, white—whatever day is on offer, a waving to the clouds, a dappling to the ground. You, feeling you are no longer of the earth, as you, too, dance in the sky, light inside, your body weightless, all heaviness left behind.

'I will stay here for a while,' I thought, the first time I found myself floating in its arms, shunned that day, by Lizzie, head in her book, thoughts elsewhere; or Lizzie and

Father, heads together, words entwined.

'I will live here, maybe.' 'I will have company.' The butterflies that rested on their way home. The birds that stopped by, the woodpeckers to chisel their holes, the jays to find their acorn-fill. Red-start, fly-catcher, nut-hatch.

Maybe the birds would bring food to me, crumbs of bread, worms. Would I eat worms? Perhaps they would share their eggs with me, nuts, seeds…

But the Oak had more sense than me, and told me, along with the cold numbing my arms, stinging my eyes, my nerves knocking and locking, my whole body sinking, to climb back down and go home. Still, it would always be my friend, I could tell it every loose thought I wanted to tell, everything I knew, I felt—and it would listen, always, no matter that it already knew.

… knowing everything, after all, what goes on now, what went before. Affairs spied by its topmost branches, or sucked in by its roots that spread through the earth, thick, thin, thinner, until no more than a single strand of cobweb, yet still burrowing, gleaning, surfacing. Seeing, therefore, what takes place from above and below. Looking back through the ages, all the years it has been there, longer than any other growing thing, time wrapped in rings inside it. Told happenings by others, other than me, whispered face to bark; written by some, against the grain. The secrets of the Ancient Ones, who worshipped at its feet; the young men and maidens who danced around it at Solstice; the ghosts who haunted it, each thinking they were alone. All these and more, baring their souls.

Something else, not known by many…

… that the Oak will tell back, will tell those it favours, if you ask nicely.

And, when I needed, when I wanted, I asked nicely.

So that I knew, too.

Raised by the wood, wood raised me… the oak, the rowan, the ash, the holly, the willow, the elder, the alder, all. The other mysteries found there, deep within, part of it, but not tree-rooted, teaching, too.

For, older still, I saw, learnt, more, lain beneath the Oak, cushioned on star moss, sprinkled with tormentil stars kept awake by the moon—Father away, Oak allowing, me, not afraid, even at midnight's hour. Knowing the night's turn, dawn's revels; willow-clutched to see in the dark. Hidden between its arms, I watched the Ancients come, witnessed their ceremonies—their cutting of mistletoe, blossom and berry, to match summer and winter solstice; their gathering of vervain, at the rise of the Dog Star, left-hand digging, waving, in the hope of foretelling. How they sacrificed to Gras Duw, a charm against misfortune, seeking it before sunrise in the open groves.

I laughed at their antics—as gaudy as my father's— laugh turning to frown, as they shaped a golden sapling into a cross, marring its bloom.

Digging deeper within, Oak left behind, I found the cot behind the bramble hedge, where the wood witch dwelled. A true witch, no hooked nose, or pointed chin, no wry teeth or chapped fingers, nor lumpen neck. One pupil in each eye, not two, to see myself upturned. No. None of these marking traits. Nor like the tricksing 'sisters', either. No more, no less than a grower of herbs, a watcher of life. I saw her kneeling down to the sun at its rising, making a triangle with her fingers, to spy the moon. Stand in the circle of the glade, silent, breathing; light a candle at the hidden stones. Hug the trees, as I did, in greeting. A friend to Mother Nature. A friend, in time, to me, too.

More friends found, in maiden guardians of the Heads, River finding them for me, leading me further up to other Falls—falls unlike my father's theatre. These, white tumblers, scrambling down the rocks, to gather. A sharp descent, a bride's veil, flowing, flowering into a rainbow, dancing on the rock walls that surround. Dancing between, over the scored lines and curves. Carvings. Shapes, misshapen, puzzled over. Stars, sun? Animal crudely drawn. Hands, traced. Other parts of the body, some of them, that I am not supposed to know.

This is where the Heads stand, one, two, three, given by the river, posited here, positing, when properly asked. The maidens guiding—the maidens who danced as lithe as the water, gracing their gods with their gifts, their worship.

I feared them, first, these stone faces, their sunken, lidded eyes, their fleshy lips, their baleful look. But the guardians blessed me, and the Falls cleansed me, and the Heads, in time, smiled, and welcomed me in, so that I danced with the maidens, too.

What else? What other is there, in the wood at night? I hear the owl, see it, a ghostly shape. I watch it killing. I see the steady sweep of its wings, then its dive. The small creatures that run over me, as I lie—these are its prey. The pale phantom carries them away in its claws. I see it rest on the branches above me, pulling at the flesh held close, its hooked beak tearing, swallowing down. Dawn, and I find the pellets shitted from it, the fur and bones still visible— my scampering friend. This is death. In life, it ran fast, eyes bright, holding the moonlight in them; its fur was velvet, its whiskers fine as gossamer as it brushed my cheek, in greeting. Yet it is a killer, too—the bugs, the worms. The way of the wood, the way of the world.

Death in life, life in death. Other ghosts, maybe, true or mistaken, no more than dreams. Blodeuwedd, passing on her way to the lake, the virgins following. A long way to run, a long way to fear. But how do you run, when you are made of flowers—oak, broom, meadowsweet—which of these were best for feet? Oak, strong, yes, but not pliant. Meadowsweet, feather-light, no good, either. Broom, then, dusting sward, splashing stream.

Broom is what I choose, when I make my own Blodeuwedd. Broom, for limbs, oak for trunk, blossom for pretty features—care taken as I weave it, making sure to stay awake, or else succumb to this, the death-flower. Da-da! Here she is—until she is caught by her wronged husband, cursed into owl—so my owl is back. Or was it never gone, no more than lost in night's deluding? No more than wood's story from long-ago?

The stories—the tales that wend through dell and grove; the witch, the Heads that rule the Falls. Better teachers than him, all; answering this question, that puzzle; this 'what if…?', that 'how can…?' My raising. 'Show me.' 'Lead me.' 'Help me.' Yes. Until…

'For cursing a man, for bringing about his death.'

We had tried many ways by then. There are lots of spells for such a needing, told by the Dyn Hysbys, whispered by the old grey men and hearth-bound women, douting the candles, as they did so. Written in books—his own books, even—leaving us wondering how often he had used them. Outside his soldiering, how many men had he killed? Or women? These, of course, I left to Lizzie, who left the other ways to me.

'Use the omens, make them work for you, driving Death through fear.' Drop his watch to the floor, so that time ends; hold the hand of the hall clock, for the same effect. Poke the longest cinder from the fire; kick the dog to make it howl.

'Did you hear that, Father? The screech of the owl? So close…' Did you hear the Cyhyraeth, as the dogs ran away?

'The cock is crowing, and it is midday. How strange!'

'Did you see that, Father? A single crow, flying over the house?'

'I saw a white crow today. Oh, I shouldn't have said…'

A white weasel.

A white pigeon. Dog. Hare. Beetle.

'A black fox! Oh, sorry, Father!'

All these will mean a death. We tried all these ways and more.

'Take a lantern, you, Lizzie, me, one in each hand.

Dress in dark colours, run through the wood, holding our hands high, fooling for corpse candles.' The Canwyll Corph.

Asking the Oak, River, any, who had always answered me before.

But… how do you curse someone themselves versed in the Black Arts, an ally of the Devil? How do you kill someone you once loved? How do you kill your father?

If that is what we did…

The word came about Lucy, first.

Words of twisted ilk, not parchment-etched, or pulpit preached.

Gossip. Tattle.

'Take a thread, any thread will do.'

Silken smooth, moistened between the lips of genteel matrons. Gobbets of fluff, hacked out from the craws of the scolds.

Gossamer yanked by the Tylwyth, dragged beneath a fringe of hart's tongue, under the buckler shields, through the mossy beards.

'Add shape and colour, warp and weft. Then bring it to your aunt/sister/coz in Cynvael Fawr.' A gift.

The word about Lucy travelled up the river, from the cot she lived in, tucked at the bottom of the valley.

It snagged on the gatepost of Tŷ Castell where my uncle Owen stood, smoking his pipe, sucking the weed and any passing words in. It snuck down the chimney of Coed Cerrig, where my cousin, Elin, sat at her weaving beside the hearth. And another yarn was spun, different from the rose tree and dove Elin happily worked on. A tale about Lucy.

Poor Lucy, foolish Lucy. Simple Lucy. *Beautiful* Lucy.

It was the word about Lucy that started it all.

Lizzie sits in the corner, her head in a book. It is what Lizzie has always done.

'Have you heard about Lucy?' I ask, sidling up, flicking the pages, so she loses her mark. It is what *I* have always done. And still do, no matter I should have grown out of such capers at such an age. She shoots hare's eyes at me—as if that would fright. Leastways she has gone beyond running to Father.

'What about Lucy?' she asks.

Lucy first came to Cynvael Fawr in the year of the famine, the year of our Lord, sixteen hundred and twenty three—an absent Lord, judged on His mercy.

A knock at our door, as soft as a fly-by-night's wing, my mother just catching it, opening.

A visitor. There was nothing strange in that, people coming, back door, front door, casement, according to need, to slant. Day or dusk, according to proper timing, too.

Our neighbour, the good Reverend, when he and my father were friend not enemy—the two of them, shut up together, with their 'man' talk, their Bible work, their learning. Others of similar inclination from further afield, border crossing.

The gypsy women to the kitchen, splaying their sprigs of heather to tempt my mother 'for luck', her falling, no matter I could bring it from the mountain in swags, no matter that heather must not come indoors. The drovers, wanting a mug of ale, as they pass. Children, wanting treats from the Big House, or tricks to thrill, if the Master is home. That coin from behind the ear. 'Father, Son and Holy Ghost, DahDah!'

And, say, 'Yes, he is at home,' there are those who come for something other, for there was this about my father, too—'Butcher, baker, candlestick-maker, healer/dyn hysbys.'

Yet another shape, another guise, confounding me when old enough to think on such a notion—strange, that a man who soldiered and hunted, killing man and beast would sprinkle time and potions to bring them back to life.

'Take a bowl of cold water, a second of melted tallow. Hold the boy's head under, counting one, two, three. Un, dau, tri. Through a carding comb, pour the tallow into the water.

Three times for this, too. One, two, three! Then pour the water onto the elder-bush, the tallow on the fire.'

Piff, paff, poof—the child's aching head will be gone!

'Joint to joint, bone to bone, so this man can stand alone!

'Blood shall rise, skin to skin, Lord, set him right, without, within!'

'Fel yr oedd Pedr yn eistedd ar faen Mynor,

'Crist a ddaeth atto, ac efe yn unig...' Etcetera, etcetera, for toothache.

Impressions seen, fancies gleaned, as I peered round the door, watching my father's finger, dipped in blood, cross Evan Price's brow, time our haymaker stuck the pitchfork in his thigh. Listening to Ezekiel's words recited one times nine, on and on about blood, polluted blood, their own blood, my blood, wast in blood. Blah, blah, blah. Seven times more, as the deep red blot spread on the ground, taking his soul with it, for wasn't that where the soul is said to be? Till Evan sunk lower, before they gathered round and carried him away.

'Where is Evan?' I asked later. 'Gone on to the next farm.'

But still they came.

Ague and colic, bone and fetlock, wrapped in skin or hide, depending, trundling across commote and cantref. 'Help me, please.'

Yes, my father is the healer of the valley—another role stolen, this from his own brother, erstwhile physician to Her Majesty the Queen. Stealing his cures from the Physicians of Myddfai, the Wise Men of the North. Working them to his own particular creed.

'Pick your supplicant, tailor your remedy, according to *your* need.'

Cutting the cloth into two: poor/peasant/simple; rich/

gentry/learned.

The frayed and ragged getting their folk charms and biblical quotes and work-a-day embrocations and balms, ministered in doorway or yard.

While the sharp-scissored and neatly hemmed (our own kind) were ushered within.

'Come in, come in!'

Nodding their heads at the book-words he spoke, borrowed from the shelves behind him. 'Humouring' with, bile, blood, phlegm dripped from his tongue (better than from them!); 'charming' with his potions.

'Drink me!'

'No, me!' Which shall it be, from the phials and flasks winking down at them?

'Fetch burdock and marsh mallow, Mared.' Fetch them from your mother's garden, before dawn. Or venture into the wood, to the witch's den, where they hang and dry—where no decent folk will go. (No, not that, but could be...)

Bubble and funnel, and seal with silver stopper. Label them in Latin or Greek.

Consult the tome, humming and hahing, choose the right tincture, poured on a silver spoon.

'Drink this, madam, sir.'

Another 'piff, paff, poof!'

And then... sleight of hand, their doing, now, not his; the silver coin slid across the desk. The king in his counting-house, fondling them into his locked chest. And I see what few see—that my father likes the finger-stroke of lucre, the crossing of his oily palm, no matter that healing should be done for free. For he wants—there is always something he wants—to build a new barn, add more rooms to the house, a new horse. New attire. And I assume, for all his skills, he has not mastered alchemy, so must turn base into gold in the traditional way. So says 'yes' to any offering, and calls it a 'gift'.

The Lord of Cynvael blesses... is blest.

Those who came in the famine could give nothing, because they had nothing to give. They came to the door, skeletons draped in skin, while Lizzie and I played 'who can count-the-most?' on their bones.

One, two, three ribs!

'You could touch them, Lizzie, wrap your thumb and forefinger around each one, no matter your hands are so small.'

Six, seven, eight vertebrae, a knotted rope down their backs.

'And their heads—look at their heads—no more than skulls, with eyes protruding.' Looking at us, licking their lips, as if we might be good enough to eat. Does Lizzie think the same?

Lizzie does not know skulls, as I do. Lizzie, who keeps inside, knowing them scrubbed and sluiced, no remnant of life. They are something else to ornament our father's lair, propping up the book-ends, mounted on stands. Sheep, cattle, fox, bird, deer, killed, bubbled, boiled, till every shred of meat is washed away. (Is the fox *my* fox—no, that, later.) A wolf—yes, a wolf!—brought from afar, or leftovers from another age, when they were spawn of the Devil, and ate any straying child?

I know other kinds, from the fields, the wood, the mountain, coming across them as I roam. A dead animal, gnawed and torn, a dishevelled corruption, taking its time.

Watching as the crows gather to the lamb, spotting it from on high, where they call to each other. 'A feast below.' Still, 'Wait!', weighting between lust and danger, swooping down, around, parrying. Afore…

Eyes, first, succulent, slippery—fighting for the easy gain. Then rip the outer hide, the tougher flesh, away to reach what lies beneath. Kidney. Liver. Heart, heart still beating, once.

So I am glad when there is nothing left but bone—bones picked clean, white bones, pure clay, so much kinder to look on than the flesh, the offal, the oozing blood, piss and shit.

Only the skull remembers life, as the creature looks up at me from hollowed orbs, pleading…

… those begged, too, the skulls outside our kitchen door, propped on their cat's cradles of bone, when the gaping mouths inside them gasped something that Lizzie and I strained to hear. Still, their stories crept over our mother's shoulder, floating on their stench, driven by their need.

'We have come across the sea,' some said. Ireland, we guessed, taught by the pedant that Ireland is to the west.

'We have walked from Scotland—' others— 'all the way from Scotland.'

We knew Scotland, too, that it was far away, and where the King-after-the-Queen came from, ruling only there, once upon a time.

We looked at their feet, saw rag-bound tattered to wisps, or bare; some scab-dressed, till drawn off by our yard's flags, staining red.

Or those not touching, hovering in air, kept aloft by a crutch of broken branch. 'From which?' my thoughts had time to wonder, wander, trusting it wasn't one of the cursing kind. As if their lives could be any worse. And yet…

'We are lucky,' they say.

This is luck?

'We are gotten away, have got this far. We are still alive. The horrors we have seen…'

… the words caught and squeezed in the jamb of the door, by my mother's speedy hand. But our ears prick sharper, snatch them back a pause along.

'… we have had to eat. Shoes boiled so's our toothless gums can chew. Rats, if they don't eat us first. For yes, we have shut our babies in tin trunks, to keep them safe. And…'

Something else? Something else they have had no choice but to eat? But my mother has pulled the door fast, now, and pushed and hushed them away. And the last words we hear are hers.

'It has been bad around here, too.'

Has it? If it has, not for us, in Cynvael-fawr. If it has, further abroad along the river, it is *nothing* like they tell.

Still…

River, afon, trickster stream, watch the river, to sign the times. Listen to what it tells. Feel it, too. Consider its fit. Dasher, sluggard; douser, dribbler. Pinch-penny, spendthrift.

No need for theatricals, a fiery orb rushing through the sky. Keep that for deluges, the death of a king, and world-ends. No need for the humdrum, the shepherd's saws. The magpie building its top-of-the-tree nest, the cuckoo perched on the may before its leaves appear. Never mind the cat sitting with its face to the fire. Or the gulls coming inland, then back again: 'Drychin, drychin, Awn I'r eithin; Hindda, hindda, Awn i'r morfa.' (But, strange, how these signs were recalled later, little mention of them at the time.)

Forget them all! Read the river, not your books, to know the skew of the year.

See the shrink of it in the winter, the fingers of ice clutching its sides, claiming its space. Hear the hush of it in summer, the leasing of it to the earth. The dwindle of the Falls, still there, always there, but less hurtle. Walk in the wood, and miss the drip of fairy tears from the hart's tongue, find the fronds dank, not weeping. Know, then, the year is a barren one.

And… this… for me, a fulness, a shape-shifting of my own, flooding blood and sweat, and tears enough, my own turn of the trick, as the deep of winter loomed.

Moon told me first, shaking me, waking me through the crack in the window-hangings, finding out the one it was looking for, aiming its mark, making ready its change. Not blinding, nor striking, nor weather-telling—a different aim, as it kept me writhing and tossing with its lanthorn glare. Giving up my sleep to it in the end, to see it full and low. The wolf's moon, howling to me, to warn me, twisting my limbs, fussing my eyes, pulling at the collar of my nightgown to let the hot breath free. I scrabble for the hem of my gown, where it gathers between my legs, chafing where all was smooth. And then… the treacle damp on my fingers, the smudge of something wet. Deeper, wetter my fingers go, then holding them up to the offered lamp, so I see, I know.

I see what the moon is telling me, how it will always tell me now—Arianrhod, the mother, guiding me—how the cramping of my belly, the lanking of my hair, my tender, sprouting breasts go hand in hand with its fullness, as it keeps me from rest.

Seeing how it does not shine on Lizzie, picking me out from the two, leaving the mere *child* alone. I, the favoured one (if not in pain, not so 'favoured' then), but happy to act the flouncing maiden, the preening madam, over her, for a chosen time, at least. Being the chosen one, for once.

Something else then, that my father went away at much the same time, and us, knowing not where, staying away for the 'now and agains' of that year. It was what he did, season on season, returning visits, or scratching the itch of the soldier's erstwhile wanderings. Or other hidden needs.

'Tuck yourselves away,' he said, before his departing. 'The winter will be a hard one this year, so shut it out, and spend your days by the fire. Yes, hibernate like the animals! The cold holds baleful humours and you are at a sensitive age.' This, to me, for yes, my mother had told him of the bleeding, leading to a discourse on the female body I had no desire to hear.

'Yes, Father,' we both sweetly simpered, bidding him 'God speed', 'farewell'; me, under my breath, 'Piss off!'

Lizzie was given back to me, then. 'So it is him that mars us,' I thought. But no, not quite, to see/speak true—how there was always something twisted between us, in the blood wending through us, or the way limb joined limb, bone found bone, muscle binding muscle, making us look at the world's offerings aslant, whether he meddled or no. Some put it simply, family, visitants, neighbours—that I took after my mother, whereas Liz took after him. Taking it at face value, our faces. Some truth in it, but more than that, always more than that.

So it was, then, as we went out into the benumbed land, for Mother was never so strict about humours, or was happily lost in hibernation of her own, revelling, perhaps, in his absence, glad of its offering of peace.

We wandered far those days, as far as the mountains, to the lake where the virgins drowned, while Blodeuwedd ran. The frost sugar-coating the tussocks, brittling the marsh beneath. A chill spot, always, drear, bleaker this year. Yet, sudden…

… this, for me, a sight of wonder—the subtle flow magicked, all water gone, ice taken its place, its edges crimped and patterned, where tussocks of grass have stitched themselves.

'Look, Lizzie, see! A fairy is trapped there, its upright wings, its mouth laughing.' The curves of its body spread wide and down, a hooped skirt, spiralling round and round. Plain as day.

Deeper, a stone is caught among the reeds. Cobwebs hang between spread fingers, clenched like a crone's arthritic hands.

'There! The face of a hare!'

'And there, spiders.' Black tresses coil from a centre. A spider caught in the ice. 'Poor creature!'

I see them all.

Lizzie puts her boot on the ice, pushes her toe around. Scritch, scratch.

'Don't.'

'Ice is frozen water. The same substance, but solid. Or

it can boil, forming bubbles. Other liquids transform, too. It is all to do with temperature, we have done experiments, Father and me, we have…'

She is mimicking my father, playing the don. She *is* my father, mirrored, but shrunk. 'It is…'

I do not need to know these reasoned facts, *her* ways of seeing.

I do not want to know.

I think of the river, chafing against my ears, helping me banish my father's lecturing, preaching, his flannel… as thick as a Welsh blanket. But there is no river here. I do what I do then, and raise my hand to my ear—'Hush, hark!'—as if someone approaches. A pretence. There is no-one, real or imagined. Blodeuwedd has gone, her companions, too, and those who chased them. There is only silence.

Except there is not. 'Listen harder.'

There is the sound of the birds, always there; the buzzards, the kites, their mewing as they wheel over the frigid landscape, searching for food. The distant cough of a sheep. The bark of a fox, out when he should be abed, on account of the freezing.

But there is more, closer at hand… or feet. It is the ice, near where I stand, sounding. A stirring, nearest the shore, where it is least tethered, where the grass frets, lacing it back. Further out, a creaking, where the hidden eddies are broken. But there is something other, if you listen harder, stop your breathing to listen, stay the harsh gasps fostered by the cold.

'Hush,' I say again to Lizzie, who looks at me strangely.

The ice is singing, a high, plaintiff air, pulling at my nerve-ends, asking something of me. A music of the spheres, yet born of earth. Nothing like, found here, not even the topmost pluck of my mother's harp. I feel myself pulled toward it, feel its despair, its wonder. I feel…

Or… is it the virgins, the maidens, their own

lamentations? Are they still here, trapped, now, beneath it? Or caught within it, where the ice reaches low.

What is worse, I wonder—for the water you float in to shrink sup by sup, or to be caught in frozen limbus, unmoving?

I see both…

… I see the maidens swimming around, arms stretched, tendrils of hair drifting, until they startle each other closer, laughing, at first, for they can hold each other's hands, a childhood chain; then closer—still pleased, for they can hug each other, until… their skin, sinews, lungs burst, dissolved into one.

Or… each one separate, fixed in the moment of freezing. See this one, her hands draped out, her mouth wide, calling. Another has wrapped herself tight, knees to chest, arms holding them, head tucked in. And there is a third, running, straining forward, her muscles locked, her face in a rictus grin.

What is she running to, or running from? Is she still running from Lleu's soldiers, who chased her here, chasing the chaste, driving her and all her fellow maidens into the lake?

Does she not realise they have long gone, if they ever existed beyond their story? But then, *she* does not exist.

It is the ice singing, nothing more, and isn't that enough? Nothing, everything, the beauty of its song.

I shake the virgins out of my head.

As Lizzie shakes them away, together with the music.

'Come,' she says. 'It's too cold for lingering and dreaming.'

We carry on, around the water, inchmeal, caught by some magic I see.

'Look, Lizzie, look.'

'Come on!'

Here and again, she will stop, peer down at what I say I am seeing, looks this way and that, scrapes with her boot, harder—on and on, round and round and round, with its sharp toe—where I am seeing a constellation of stars, their points interlocking, beaming towards me.

'Don't!'

But she won't hark, scouring the white powder from the surface, working her toe deeper. The stars cloud over, the picture fractures, along with the ice. A jagged mosaic takes its place—another pattern, but not the one I liked.

Another sound, now, human, not belonging. Like, but not like, the shouts of the maidens, as the water welcomed their bodies. This, no more than a foot, Lizzie's foot, following her boot through the ice, the ice-cold water creeping through the stitches and over the top.

'Arghh!'

The gentlest of nudges is all it takes, so gentle she doesn't know.

My punishment, too, that we have to go home. Still, it is good to see her screwed up face, her chattering teeth, her blue skin, as she hops along.

Still, I am sad the stars are lost, hearing the mirror of the lake shattering behind me.

Snow follows soon, falling on frozen ground. My father still gone. We go again, up again, my mother's words shrugged away. 'Take better care of your sist-uhhh.'

The mountains are what you seek in the snow… *I* seek.

It is Lizzie's first time without Father to hoist her on his shoulders, the first time she must walk in the drifts.

We have wrapped skins around our calves, fur between them and our boots.

'Walk in my footsteps,' I tell her, then lengthen my gait beyond her stride.

The mountains are blue today, stealing the colour of the sky. This is what they do, I have seen, ever-changing, a tapestry of rainbow hues. Blue, at this moment, with white swags. A black smudge, here and there, marking the deepest crevices. The snow has let those be.

I want to climb them, I want to go to the highest

point, to look down over the white land. This is more snow than I have ever known—who has always known it on these mountains, seeking them out with each fall, as soon as I was old enough, but never seeing them like this.

But 'this' is deeper than our fur-bound calves, will soon be deeper than Lizzie's waist, and we can go no further. Or she can't. If it weren't for her, I would go, somehow. I would thread together twigs from the forest, freely given, to make shoes to ride on. I would tie pattens to my hands, and 'swim' through. I would…

But no, we must turn for home, to stop Lizzie's whining, though I will not let her deprive me entirely.

'The wood is an easier way,' I say.

There is little snow here, in the heart of the trees. Yet, looking up, I see a filigree of frosting traced across the highest boughs. Closer, iced moon milk hangs down, reaching for me, offering itself to me. I stretch, and play my fingers across their swollen teats. They chime, then break, their moon dust spiralling to the ground.

Lizzie shakes herself and glares at me.

'Stop it.'

I reach again, loving the sound made—nothing else.

'Stop!'

We trip on.

Lace drapes over the hawthorn, its left-over berries studding like glass beads. A thing of beauty, nature-made, there is so much beauty here… then…

A bird perches on a frosted bough, dead. My father's birdlime, that he daubed in autumn, aiming to catch more fodder for his cage, his tricksing. Thoughts against him come more with my growing, changing. But when I look higher, beyond where he could climb, I see more birds, clammed to the bark, fixed. Are they all dead? Do I imagine that the eyes of the finch are moving, the wings of the robin fluttering? Their shadow-shapes stand above the black bones of the branches, or the washed-out sky behind. There is no green, now. The colours of the wood have drained from it, lost in the dying of the year, the birds.

I pull Lizzie away, from the dead birds, the dead bird tree, not wanting to see the dead flesh any longer. Yet, as soon as I am gone from it, were they there, or no more than motes before my eyes?

Where the trees thin and the snow drapes the floor, the prints of live animals litter the ground, caught until melting.

'They are out early, searching for food,' I tell Lizzie, wanting her to know about the wood, the river, the mountain in a different way from Father's teaching. There are different ways to know.

'These are animals that do not hibernate. See.'

Or… do they have fathers who tell them to stay inside, but choose not to listen, wanting to see this new world, their wood in snow?

I tell the animals from their prints, reciting 'fox, deer, rabbit'. I watch the way they go, and start to follow. 'Like hands, for the squirrel—this will take us to its tree. The long toes of the deer, mimicking the ears of the doe. The…'

'No,' Lizzie tells me. 'I want to go home.'

She wants to go home, back to poke her head inside a book, to see what it tells her, instead of my words, instead of looking around, reading what the earth says, the trees, the creatures of the wood. This is what *he* has taught her. This is all *she* wants to know. This is how she wants to see. A different way to mine.

The wheel of the year turns its first spoke. I wake one day to find half the wood gone—the earth-girt bottom, the girth of trunk, the root. Above, the latticed twigs still live, criss-crossing against the sky. But beneath…

'Wake up, Lizzie. Something has stolen the thick of the wood. A river nymph, maybe, or a wight.'

She rubs her eyes, blinks at me, a cat disturbed from sleep, this time; pushes and pulls herself to the window.

'It is mist,' she says. 'Dullard. Mist caused by the moisture, warm meeting cold, from the river valley. Mist, as is always there, due to the high volume of water vapour. And shut that window, 'fore the fever blight descends on us all.'

I wake another day to find the wood half gone. The fine-wrought skein, between the girth and the clouds. The broomstick branches and whips all wiped away.

'Wake up, Lizzie. Something has stolen the tops of the trees. A giant, maybe, come to cut them down in the night. Or the ghost of a traitorous woman. The Princess of the North. Blodeuwedd!'

She turns in her bed, away from me, and pulls her blankets over her head.

'No more,' she says. And yes, that is it, as she pays attention to our father's words, and burrows deep for the rest of the winter, leaving me to solitary rambles, and warped ways of looking of my own. Happy enough, maybe.

Spring came and went, Father back, then gone again. Come, with stories of lack and want in every place he had been to. Gone, because he had 'important matters to attend to.'

Snow-melt swelled the river, then travelled along it to the sea. The new growth faltered through lack of rain. The land warmed, too much, too soon.

We could go out, at last, without strapped skins—bonnets, for the sun. Better for fussing children, a fussing child. Lizzie. No hibernating, surely.

'Come on, Liz! Come out and enjoy the sun!'

No, no, no. Head in book, again, wanting more of the praises Father had heaped on her, during his return. 'You have progressed so well, my dear.'

Still, sometimes, she would come; sometimes, we would move in harmony, hands held, even; heads together, playful…

… even, once in a blue moon, unwaith yn y pedwar amser, joining together against our father, just as we were to do, in the end, his end.

That was when we found the stone in the Cynvael— no, on the edge of the river, but where its water should be. The stream was narrowing, now it had lost so much to the sea, the parch. Its banks were growing into cracked mud, littered with secrets from beneath.

Creatures mouth-gaping, flapping, their homes washed up on land. The kingfisher on its branch, a squint in its look, as it eyes the shallows below. If we went to the lake, would we find the maidens sitting on its shore, gawping around, wondering what world they had come to? Dry, when they were used to wet—become a startled, useless flotsam.

But there was no lake that day, or the next—finding the stone, judging its size and the hollow near one end. The thought coming to both of us, at once, as one.

We marked the spot with a cross, worked at it, with chisel and flint, stolen from the barn, laughing over it, between huff and puff, until…

'There!' A hole through it, just where it should be, level with a tall man's chest. 'Done! First step!'

Done. But this is what we must do, next—tug, pull, pull, tug, huffing and puffing, more. 'Push!' All to no avail.

'We need a lever. A branch from an oak!'

But, no. No good, still.

We are not strong enough, nowhere near, how could we be, two half-fledged girls? But there was Mal, the cow-hand, strong as an ox, ready to do any we bid him, for a smile and an apple. Happy to push a slab of rock half-back under the stream, without question asked.

'Hush, Mal, our secret!'—another rise of our lips, a finger to them. 'Hush!'

'Look, Father, look,' we tell him, as soon as he returns. 'Look what we found while you were gone.' Dragging him to the river, one on each side.

'Look at the size of it. See the hole through it, where it is. What can it be but Gronw's shield, this surely being the place?'

My father looks at the stone, we look at him, see the gleam in his eyes, seeing him running his fingers round the jagged opening, his, our breath stopping…

… our breath coming again, as he speaks. 'Proof, if proof were needed. This is, indeed, where the killing happened. Where Lleu threw his spear at Gronw. Just here, on the bank of the Cynvael. Just as we always believed. 'Llech Ronw'.'

I listened to my father, his voice telling it, making up the scene. I listened to it carved and honed, with each telling; told to all who would listen, as they were taken to the spot and shown the stone. A stone *he* had found, Lizzie and I forgotten.

This is what can happen with tales. They can be turned, and turned again. All you have to do is believe.

Summer—a summer stuck fast in the deepest rut of the Wheel, River shrivelling, fish gone further down, towards where it yawned again, towards the sea, ruled by moon, not sun. Told by the cuckoo, before the blackthorn leaved.

Grass faded from elven green to dead furze, to be scuffed away by beasts, their hooves, their muzzles nuzzling deep for the scarce fodder. Soon, it was no more than dust, to be blown away, up, up, the mountains, and into the air beyond. The beasts themselves diminished, their stomachs gnawing and tightening, their bones growing through their skin.

This, on the farms further up, where the earth gave away nothing, fixed with stone, where the river was narrowest, deep-running, and fed less.

This, for those farms—not us, with our stone barns stored with grain and hay, with Father's chests of money—gold buying anything, even what isn't there.

If those who walked here from Scotland, who escaped the eating of… what?… called themselves 'lucky', what were we? Luckier still.

'We will give them something, won't we?' we asked our mother, thinking of those full barns and coffers.

And yes, we gave them something—hunks of stale bread, our black-eyed potatoes, scrag-ends of meat.

Yet they were grateful, as if we had placed a king's banquet in front of them.

'We have to be careful,' said our father, home again, who answered the door now. 'You have been too generous, my dear. We don't know what's coming. Or… I do know, if it is as I've borne witness to. We have to think of our neighbours, how we might need to help them. And we have to parcel fairly. So many more may come. We must make sure we keep back, to have something for everyone.'

And yes, more came, more of the same, or much the same, day after day, so that we began to think there was truth in his words, his withholding, no matter how our hearts bled, as their weary stick-legs carried them on their way.

And then there was Lucy.

'Come in,' our father cooed, the day she appeared in a halo of sunlight, heralded by a chorus of tweeting songbirds, while the flowers opened their faces in awe—or was it no more than our blinded eyes?

'Sit down. Sit by the hearth, put your feet on this stool. I will bathe them for you.'

Him, not the scullery maid, nor even my mother, with Lucy's feet better than many come before, the flesh still clinging to their bones.

'An ointment for treating broken skin, a bleeding wound,' he chanted. 'Take a ...'

We looked on, Lizzie, mother and me, while he moved around the kitchen, preparing his ingredients.

'Add a sprinkling of...' dripping sugar all the while.

We watched, as he knelt down before her, picked up her feet, first one, then the other; her pale, long feet, bathing them, first, to wash the dirt away, the tender sponge wending from toe to ankle, ankle to toe. Saw his working between each toe, while the soap frothed in the bowl, then flecked on her skin. Looked as he patted them dry, soft, gentle, with our own precious bath cloths, then dipped his fingers into the silken salve, rubbing round and round and round, gazing at her face, into her eyes, all the while. Rubbing further up her legs, then, 'for this is a cure for many ailments, to work the hands, thus.' To work them, all over.

Lucy, we decided, skulked behind the dais screen, was a year, perhaps, older than me. Later, we learnt she herself did not know. It was the same with much of her story, full of rents, slipped stitches, tangles—so that *we* did not, could not, know. There was always something 'other' about Lucy, including her beauty.

I gave her my clothes, too big for her in girth, on account of her starving, too small for her in height—but making do, with a tuck and a pull here and there.

It was strange to see myself as I would be, if quite a different person. If I were beautiful...

She was to stay with us for a few days, which became a few weeks, while we fed her, made her well—Lucy 'having nowhere else to go', no matter that there were so many with nowhere to go. Lucy was always different.

Strange, that my father, who had been absent for so much of that year, with 'pressing business' elsewhere, should be home those weeks.

Strange, that Lucy had ills unseen, needing his healing hands, before the needs of all other visitants, any of our neighbours.

We were too untutored to understand such mysteries, we assumed. We looked, we wondered, but nothing more.

Besides, we liked Lucy, who smiled at us, as she smiled at everyone, with the same moon-struck gaze in her big, bottomless eyes—azure pools where silver motes met sunbeams, dappling together in their depths.

We took her with us, that summer, on our ramblings. *I* took her with me, for now that father was home again, Lizzie was minded to stay inside, wanting his discourse and his books, instead of 'outdoor nonsense'.

So I was glad of Lucy's company, which was always easy, and in spite of all her ills, she was soon fit enough to keep up with me.

I showed her the river, the wood, the mountains; I told her the tales. Some, she already knew from her grandmother, she said. Others goose-walked-over-her-grave, as I spoke, and I wondered, later—much later—if she already knew what was in store for her. But still she smiled at me, or held my hand as we went, which Lizzie hadn't done for many a year.

At eventide, Father would tend to her again, and then we would all sit round the hearth, when Mother would play her harp, while he recited his poetry. And Lucy looked at him, for words always thralled her—these rhyming words more than any, wrapping her in their lilt and song. And he looked at her. Or was it no more than a cozen of the firelight? Or another thing remembered after the event, after all that happened?

Late at night, I would hear noises from below. He had encountered new theories on his recent journeyings, he explained when I questioned him. He needed to think on them longer, to investigate them further. Nothing more than this.

And then Lucy was to go, announced one morning, for no seeming reason, beyond my mother's voice raised through closed doors. A 'place' had been found for her. Mrs. Morgan, further down the cwm, needed a 'girl', her own daughter having recently wed. A cot the other side of Uncle Owen's house. Not too far, not too near.

'You shall still be able to see her,' Father said, as we fared her well and God speed.

And yes, I still saw Lucy. Saw her as her bones softened, her shape curved, her hair grew thick and golden, all mark of dearth gone. The mothers and grandmothers shaking their heads at the look of her, muttering the trouble such looks could bring. The boys thereabouts called by the word, mooning around her, searching for signs and spell to turn her their way. The girls cross at her coming, where she did not belong, giving them no chance, where luck should be theirs.

Not me, nor Lizzie, who had known her when she came, who knew her for far more than her looking, who knew how simple she was, meaning the word for what it simply was. There were no airs to her, no gall. Nothing, in truth, beneath those looks. Except a heart.

A year, or maybe more, passed, time not always heeded then. The lack had eased, here and abroad. Lizzie, too, was found by the Moon. The King died—that was certain—but not all his leaning with him. Satan, his minions and the Black Arts had seeped from his thoughts to fester and spread.

The witches, hereabouts, had Fortune on their side, by custom, escaping the full wrath of God, King, Country and the Just found in other parts. My father and his punishments were the worst of their woes, as far as any knew. Their secret devices in the depths of the wood, on the hidden slopes of the mountains were seldom revealed.

Father came and went, went and came, bringing new sounds from the depths of the house, louder, deeper than before. Hammer-blows and chinking, as of the miners and their knockings, as he knocked and chiselled the cellar into a new 'study', separate from his library. 'A place to conduct my new investigations, fostered by my recent learnings.'

When I slipped down there, after midnight, queer lights and curious smells accompanied the sounds creeping under the door.

Even Lizzie was forbidden to enter there.

'Is it Alchemy he has taken to?' I asked her. 'Is that what he has 'learnt' on his travels?'

'And what if it is? There is nothing wrong in it. It is all for the good—or would be with Father. It is, after all, an ancient philosophy, long practised in the furthest realms of the Earth...'

A lecture. I was going to have one of her lectures, and yes, she carried on, me, half-listening to her words.

'... China, Egypt...

'... to purify and perfect base materials, in order to create a panacea for disease...'

A book lecture this, for surely she was quoting from one of those deadly tomes.

'... and new laboratory equipment and techniques would be needed for such experimentation, hence this additional room... and substances such as sulphur, mercury—quicksilver—that is much needed...

'... it is, after all, a holy discipline, much linked to the Christian... and to heal...

'... the Queen...'

Enough.

'Yet he does not need you.' Knowing this would stall her, as I left the room.

Otherwise, we carried on, much as ever, she and I

always better together when he was away, though she spent much of her time, as ever, in the library, her head in those books, 'the best books of the best minds in this land and all lands, from now and before,' as she was always saying.

And yes, on occasion, those who came to the door, wearing their workaday-ills, would allow her to treat them, from what she had learnt therein—those who thought Lizzie more able than the witch in the wood, regarding my father's potions, lotions and charms more powerful than the herbal lore from the mists of time, offered by the land around.

Yet their faith in Lizzie was always tempered—me, seeing their shoes shuffle, their wondering when 'Master' would be back. Seeing their own sleight-of-hands, as they slipped her phials into their pockets, then out again, tossing them over the nearest hedge.

There were times when I rescued their cast-offs, and hid them away, changed from the 'once-upon-a-time' when I would rush back to Lizzie, to wave my findings in front of her eyes, gloating and goading. But we were older, now. Besides, it irked me that their credence faltered on account of her sex. A woman could bury herself deep in the forest, leaving her charms to be plucked from a tree, but who was this slip-of-a-thing madam, spouting instructions, offering ministrations, wrapped up in preaching words? And the seventh daughter of a seventh son was never seen as good as, lacking full pedigree, 'without alteration of sex' being much preferred.

Mind, that she saw none of it for herself, and preened about the house, eating my sympathy away.

Still, I minded her nonsense less, idling my days out of doors, allowed to wander further up, down, and betwixt.

And there was always Lucy to call on, should I want company—always glad to see me, making time for me, no matter how many young men were waiting outside the gate for a smile, given readily to all.

There were diversions we found, then, the two of us,

deep in the wood, that we kept close. There were many sports done in the deep of the wood, kept close by those who did them.

But there were other pastimes for myself alone, for Lucy, after all, must do her work for Mrs Morgan, whereas I was let be. And I spent my days by the river, paddling in the river, or beneath the surface of its pools, learning its grown-up ways, seeing it anew. My Cynvael.

Cupped hands, water scooped, seeped through finger-flesh, palm-binds—sipped—my river. But what? Where? Wanting to hold it fixed in more than hands, to put it in mind, heart, as if that would show. End in the beginning, beginning in the end. All.

Up, first, I went, following its crimping sides. Up, up, plain to see, me, climbing, banks steeping below, rising to mountain. Feet sinking, dragging, cloying, through clagging earth. But… a backward glancing, vast called… gone! Lost! Down, squelched, knees muddied and bowed, eyes close, I saw the swallowing ground. Down, turned on its head, not as it should—its uprising, its spring, its springing from the depths of the earth. Where?

Fingers spread, delving, following the rindle beneath tussock, slate, stone. Here. Here! 'This is where it begins,' drinking from its clear spawning, its own birth; my birth, its birth, together now. Or maybe not (for isn't that another welling a rock's cast away?). But it will do. It will more than do, letting its silver liquid dribble over my lips, then drinking it deep. What does it taste of? It tastes of the depths of the earth, and all that it must pass through, to reach the air—fire, the blood-red stone, the cleansing white, all. Warming and freezing both at once, as it reaches the pit of my belly.

I wash it over my hands, my arms, my face, feeling its

virtue, my skin quickening at its touch, my eyes brightening straight.

Yes, this is its beginning, its well head, I decide. A well rises here, used by the folk from long ago who wandered these mountain tops, to quench them, to nourish them—to heal them. I think of them worshipping here—their own gods—giving thanks, for this gift, the blessing of pure water, making their offerings. Or… did the fairies own it, living beneath it—I step away, at that thought—or the witches, using it for their own purposes, good and bad. Cursing…

Any of these, all of these. All I know is what I decree—that this is the beginning of my river, the source of all its goodness. Begun.

Begun…

… end, ending   not so easy to find. Yet 'down' I knew I must go.

… down…… wider……… flaring, the spread of that wedge, knowing the sea was the answer, my river's conclusion. Yes?

The sun led me, the longest I had travelled. Day after day, foot in front of other, no more than a bag of bread and cheese laid in, more begged from passing dwellings, claiming kin to the valley's Master—already guessed by most.

It was those who told me, first, beached on broadest stream. Shaking their heads at my intent, pointing their fingers, mouthing a name. 'Dwyryd.'

Not my river, not my Cynvael—or Cynfal, they said. A thief, a bully. Dwyryd.

Them, holding hand on palm of the other, not saying, not knowing it for the letter 'T'. 'Dwyryd'. 'Crossing'. Mouthed as if to one who could not comprehend.

I walked in the stream, deeper, here, water chafing at my knees, feet sinking in silt, more than tripping on stone; bank right, bank left, same. Cynvael, Cynfael, Cynfal, call it what they/you will. Same. Except… another bank, now, across, ahead, that top etch of the T.

Did my river turn both ways? Or was the talk true? Shapeshifter stream, countering the gouged earth, or air, full of nothing to see or feel.

Cup hands, once more, lift it to me. But where is 'it' from? Where goes it now, leaching through my fingers? Dripping back down into… what?

Where is Cynvael? Where is its end?

Here, about my knees, or there, a pace forward? Bound unseen?

Or mingle, muddle, Cynvael in Dwyryd, Dwyryd in Cynvael, chop, slop, plash, spill, spew, babble, ripple into one? Dwyryd gulping, swallowing—bigger.

No. No witching for Cynvael. Cynvael stays. Like the Dee through Llyn Tegid—no mixing.

This… where my foot lifts from the bottom's ooze— the pooling there.

River's edge, lapping, overlapped. Can be Cynvael, if I say. Cynvael carrying on, a turn taken, that way, to the sea.

Following Cynvael down, working its way through the Dwyryd, down, down to the sea. River's true ending, if I say.

River widening as I walk beside it, or bank drifting away, away. Dimmed, distant, another land, river bounding, another's fiefdom, then lost into something else again.

A bay, eyes stretched both ways, then narrowed again. A channel, snaking, breaking, tree-lines gone, magicked into rough, tough grass, mountain tussocks transplanted. Sand. Gold dust, another thing to cup, then run away. But the channel spreads, stays wider, out, out, more, more. Arms stretched wide, beyond stretching. The sea, the sea!

Perhaps.

For… another conundrum… where does river end and sea begin? Or sea end and river start, depending? Another coming-and-going, 'twixt and 'tween, only more. Water still the Cynvael? Or Dwyryd, other depending?

Or…

No. This is the sea, certain, seen close for the first time, seen from afar, before. Him, showing it from the mountains, showing the mark of his territory.

'Look, the sea.'

Turned west, him lifting me high, I saw a saucer of blue, no more. Clouds came, turning it grey and green, a shade-shifter, daubed by the sky. That was all, then.

And now this.

Blue, still, not river hue, lapis-deep. Yet white flecked, where I stood. I had not known waves, from far away, from a distant mountain. Wash-day froth capping the water, riding to shore, to me. Fierce, then fraying, then backing away—all strange. Small water-horses? True, the river roiled in flud, breaking over the stones, turned thick, peat-brown, or yellow-white, or bride-white at the Fall, as surface shattered and dissolved.

Yes.

But this, where there were no rocks to crash on, no giddy cascade. A hidden might? The wind? But there was none. A god? But which?

A being powerful enough to turn water into sand, sand into water, back and forth, forth and back.

For this happened—feet in water, feet on land, again and again. An impish trap, catching me, wetting those feet. Why?

'The sea…' The Master of Cynvael, the Master of the Sea, too, by own reckoning. 'This is caused by…' he says, crouched on the shore, hands in water. Words of reason explaining, not wanted in river, wood, mountain. But here, maybe, to show what 'end' was. For who else could tell me?

'There—what is that?' me, pointing, puzzling at the line drawn between sea and sky, to be lost to another mingling at the edge of the world.

'Is the sea turning into the heavens, or the heavens returning to the sea? Becoming one?'

Land, in this moment, had won, threat turning to

tease, as it hushed. My breath came more easily, my legs grew stronger, as if fear had left. Had I been afraid? Thinking the ocean would pull me under, claim me for itself, turning me into a mermaid, or some such underwater slave.

'Why?' I ask again.

I knelt beside him, if he were there, filled my hands, showing him, feeling its weight, against the river. Looking closer, I saw silt, waving shreds of green. Sea weed, weed of the sea, that I had walked through on the shore, slicked by the ocean, black, green, red, brown; sleek ribbons, lacy tendrils, suckered flesh. Other—scraps, scrapings discarded, remnants of shells, or creatures smaller than a grain of sand.

'Would your glass show more, transforming a speck into legs, eyes, bodies?'

Changing water into something else, as he changed everything.

Alchemy.

Shape shifting shape shifter.

Maybe.

But, instead, gone. He magicks it away.

(No, not him, he is not here, remember?)

Like River, it crept through the crevice of my palms. Like River, it always finds a way. Water…

'Taste it,' he said, as I cradled it, once more.

Making me spit, and splutter, and shake it from my mouth. Teaching me with deeds, this time, not words—the salt of sea-water. Enough to crack lips and gag throat. River was not for drinking, I knew well enough, having opened my mouth to it and swallowed it down, in foolish embrace. Only at its beginning, where it came from the earth, was it pure enough to imbibe. And here, at its end, NO.

But it was not its end, I had learnt, or ruled it thus. The Cynvael, my Cynvael, was long gone. And I was glad.

I would keep the Cynvael close—what was close would be the Cynvael. Short, sharp Cynvael, it would be.

The spring to the reach of the Dwyryd. No more. Enough.

I would let this sea be. I would let it keep its mysteries. I would keep my father quiet, his words unsaid.

'Farewell,' banishing the sea from my life, banishing his words, his steering, another 'no more', another 'enough'. The river, the wood, the mountain, me, them; *their* teaching.

Turning. Walking away, back to them. Walking along… River.

The sun shifts, the moon waxes, wanes, round and round. Same as, or not. Father gone, or not, until—'I will not go again.'

'I have been in foreign lands, and spent time with certain great men. In England, too. I have gained much new knowledge, in spite of all I knew before. There are deeds to be done, ways to be examined, for the future, in readiness.' Bringing back brows locked together, furrows around his eyes. Less meat.

'Is he thinking of dying?' I asked Lizzie. But Lizzie would not countenance such thoughts, not then, and threw a slipper at me.

'It is simply that his new wisdom must be tested. That is all he means.'

'Is that why he spends more time in his secret room, in the depths of night?' Doing…

'What? What does he do down there, Lizzie?' Knowing to rattle her, she, still, forbidden there.

'I am too busy committing his new studies to paper. That is what he wants of me, just now. I will, no doubt, take part in his new experiments in due course—will be taught to undertake such scrutiny myself.' Said, in her clipped tones, her precise words—how she spoke more and more.

Said, as if I cared, but no, I did not. Laughing, instead.

'And what if you were not to like what you find there?'

Leaving her, mouth half open, word half out.

These signs speak to me—the stroke of fingertips, the cleft in the dust, a gasp in the air, showing me loose bricks in the hearth, creaking floorboards, hollow books, giving me the key, letting me in.

And think, at first, it is no more than his library, drawn twice. Drawn darker, a line crossed, faint, at first, then getting bolder. Seeing, holding my candle close. The pages of the books revealed, but not. His writing, what I knew, but didn't know, lines, hooks, arcs, numbers? Maybe. Symbols… of what? They are there, too, on the floor, my eyes lightening the dark, magnified. A circle, pentacle-crossed, signed at each point. Another, divided by other shapes. A table, with bowl and bellows, a three-legged stand holding a spherical jar. Charts line the walls, of unfathomable meaning.

Bottles and tubes glint from the shelves, their contents glowing, dimming with the flicker of the flame. One, blood, I am sure it is blood.

And I am watched. Big, round, empty eyes staring down at me. There is nothing behind them. Skulls. But these are human, these are not allowed.

Where do they come from? Where has he found them? Each and every to be boxed beneath the ground, those who belong to no-one, included—left unmarked, beyond the churchyard wall, away from the godly, Christian parishioners, but still in the earth. A home of sorts. It is done, yet here they are. Men and women, side by side, woman-kind snaring me, most.

'This… me.' I touch my face to map the shape in front of me, fingers pressing through skin and meagre flesh. Feeling the contour of my cheek, the arch of it up, the circle of bone around eye. I stroke my jaw—the mirror'd wired to hold in place—up, down, flexing my mouth, reaching the hinge between.

'This is me, but it cannot be. This is not what I want.'

Seeing what I wish not to see, being where I should not be—that first time, I turned and ran...

... they, following on, as I tossed and turned, back in my own bed, half-wake, half-sleep. Dreamt. A circle of heads, dancing around me, leering, without tongue, without lip. And then my father was there—a churchyard, now—shovelling the earth from an unmarked grave. I, they, watched as he scrambled, scrabbled on his hands and knees, scraping at the wooden lid, hiding what lay within. Wood split, heard, if you can hear in dreams, seen, splintering away, and him, lifting a body out of the box, out of the grave, flesh dripping, as he carried it away. Taking it, bringing it...

Here.

I woke, hot and cold together, clawing at the bed sheets, thinking of the body beneath me, sure it was there. It, with others. What did he do with them? I had seen a table, the length and width of a man. I saw the corpse laid there. I saw...

I shook such thoughts from my head. I had been asleep. I had been dreaming. I had been mistaken.

Bone. That was all.

Tap, tap. The knock is quieter, coming in the witching hour, no more than a brush of knuckles, maybe, or the touch of a whip. I am not supposed to hear, I am not supposed to know there are visitors in the time of the dead. But he must know they are coming, must be waiting for that touch, for the door opens, as if charmed.

From my window, I see them slide in through its narrow opening, wrapped in cloaks and darkness. My turn to slip—to the top of the stairs that lead to the cellar. This is where they will be, where all the people of the night go. Who are they? What do they want? Why do they not come in the daytime, when decent folk appear, coming for all those things he gives them, in all the roles he plays. Blessings, rhymes, charms, healing—laws—all these can be ministered from dawn to dusk. What is different here? What do they seek, what does he give?

I put my ear to the door, but it is hewn of ancient oak, fitted well. Still… a chanting, a single note, sometimes, that rises in pitch. A scream. One night, I think I hear a scream, the scream of a girl, but maybe I am mistaken, yes, surely I am wrong. I place my eye to the keyhole, like any sneaking child, but he, the Queen's spy, has locked it from the other side, and left the key in place.

Toriad-y-dydd—they will go before it, when all the creatures of the night fly back to their lairs. I wait at the top of the cellar steps, hidden behind the drapes. But they are still no more than shadows, fleeing through their conjured mist.

'Wake up, Lizzie, wake up!'

See what I have seen, catch those shadows as they melt into the wood. Tell me what they are.

But no, I let her sleep. Something holds my lips, trapping the words inside. Something worries in my head, twists and turns in my stomach. These are happenings I do not want her to know, as if… I seek to protect her. Strangest of all.

Yet, is she not to be taught everything, if she is his successor, the one who will carry on his work?

And yes, there is this, that she scribes morn to eve, but *this* changed—bent over the kitchen table or our bedroom dresser; not shut in the library, or tucked in a corner, or arm shrouding her book, as she was wont before.

No need—for when I pull her arm away, or look over her shoulder, what is there tricks my eyes and fogs my brain, turving my mind. Words written backwards, from top to bottom, maybe. Numbers, maybe, or maybe not, lines this way and that, higgled and piggled, or widdershins.

'Code,' Lizzie says, eyes and mouth screwing together.

'Father wants me to use code now. A secret language, so no-one can steal his work. It is a skill he learnt long ago, while in the army, used for secret communications. Or spies. It is wise to use such hidden terms for this. It is not for the uninitiated, for the wrong hands. But with him…'

I have seen such writing before, or similar, in the books opened in the cellar, letters pulled from hidden drawers. Some signed by gentlemen I know, living no more than a day's ride away. Why, therefore, do they write in this secret fashion? What is it they plan?

I would like to wipe her catty-cream look off Lizzie's face. Time was when I would, time after when I twisted the skin on her arm, or pinched the white flesh inside her wrist. Time when I would drop a morsel or dangle a promise from my store of gleanings, to see her eyes cloud, her brows pucker, her quill stall above her page. But no, not with this. Not with this latest transformation of our father, manifest since his return. Not with human skulls, demon visitors, cries. As if I knew, already, this was something we would need to deal with together. But what was 'this'? Why? And when?

Knock, knock, again. A rat-a-tat-tat, or a nervous knuckle. A new kind of visitor, showing themselves in daylight-best, spruced up, cap in hand. Shoes-shone, hair-oiled, face red. One after the other, paraded through like prize pigs. Father flicking the switch. Father reciting their names, their pedigrees, their champion traits. Father, in a new cap, too, feathered, lined and buckled, doffed, too, to usher them in, towards where Lizzie and I wait, primped and primed, according to his instruction, Mother playing sleeping dog, somewhere behind. This new cap, his new role, sprung from lord and Master, another begun on his latest return. Matchmaker, union builder, marriage broker—all his own working, us, not asked. Lizzie and I the same, for once, no favour shown. Money, acres, blood all sought to increase his sway, nothing else considered.

So they come, according to their rote; Lizzie and I playing the game. Smiling, curtseying, waiting on them, in place of the maids, showing our best sides.

'You must serve on the left, Mared,' Lizzie whispers. 'So that the light from the window catches the swathe of your hair!'

'Make sure you wear your blue dress, Lizzie. It brings out the colour of your eyes.'

We exchange these jests, after they depart, heads together, laughing together, our thoughts as one. Playing young maidens, sisters, well enough.

'What do you think of Idris?' Lizzie asks, sitting at the mirror, brushing her hair.

'He is handsome enough, but...'

We laugh again, recalling his blond hair, his green eyes, his strong nose, '... his rosy lips! Imagine kissing them, Mared!'

No, there is nothing wrong with Idris's looks, just that there is nothing behind that strong brow.

'And Henry, who knows so much, who didn't stop talking, who was quite equal to Father in all subjects discussed at the table...'

'But the thought of those bones clunking against your flesh...'

'... your teeth coming against those yellow, rotting molars!'

'Uhhh!'

We, teasing over looks, minds, manners, while our father sits in his counting-house, calculating worth of neighbour over neighbour, cousin against cousin, this one more than that one. The spider in its web, pulling its threads, weaving them close.

'Perhaps I will not marry, if those are the ones on offer. I shall join the head-worshippers, or ask the wood-witch if I can live with her. Perhaps we will remain virgins, you, like your namesake. Anything would be better than those two, or Elwyn, Meirion or John.'

Laughing again in unison, making merry.

'Perhaps I will take a lover, if he forced a husband on me, that I did not love. Like Blodeuwedd and Gronw. Or perhaps, if we are lucky, he will die before it has to happen…'

Words said, before thinking, moment gone, marring the mood. For Lizzie, for all she is agin his machinations, cannot countenance such an event, shaking her head, her hands pulling at her sleeve, her teeth biting her lip—her childish tics.

And I do not, cannot shut up. 'Perhaps that is why he wants it settled—us, gone to another big house, with another big man to rule over us. He says he is older now, has said it much since he came back. Maybe it is something he knows.'

'No, no! It is nothing like that. Consider how busy he is with all his new enterprises. There is so much he is wanting to do.'

More words I want to say, to be uttered without deliberation, but, no, I grasp them back, hold them to me, tight. And our talk fades with the embers in the hearth, along with our good humour.

Thoughts came, in its stead, as we lay in our beds, waiting for sleep. Thoughts prompted by our hearts, our bodies beneath our blankets—or the elderflower remedy we had drained beforehand—drifting into dream, half wake, half drowsing. It was not that we were against love, after all. It was not that we wanted to stay pure.

We saw our own desired, calling them up in our nocturnal reveries, my heart beating faster as Owain Evans bent over me. Lizzie, stirring beside me, at the memory of Rhun Tŷ-Canol riding past more than his need.

We had sought out their names on the Spirit nights, as all love-struck maidens do, taught by the aged dames, knitting their stockings in the fireside-corners of the settles, whispered by the wood-nymphs, across the stream; Lizzie ignoring her books, for once, Lucy with us, welcome.

Seeking for hairs beneath the holly tree, cutting an apple in two. Foolish fal-alling, secretly hoping. Out at dawn, abroad at noon, shadow shadowing at midnight. For this…

'Dyma Twca

'Lle mae'r wain?'

'Here's the knife, where's the sheath' said seven times, as around the church we went, praying the coffin wouldn't appear.

Or this—the hardest of all, on Nos Wyl Ifan, hunting Llysiau Ifan. But 'catch your glow-worm first, your living lanthorn to light your way'. Us, dashing pell-mell up hill, down dale, Lucy leading, reaching, grasping it in the palm of her hand, triumphant, then burrowing beneath the fern, to find the plant. Lucy, good at seeing without, in place of within. Lucy, happy, at our praise.

And, look, further along the river, down the valley, see Lucy also lying in her bed, dreaming of her lovers. Or not. For we were not the only ones wooed and courted and proffered. But with Lucy, blood, wealth, connections were all as inconsequential as the fire-fly's light. It was simply… her.

Rumour, a glimpse in the market crowd, a distant sighting from the road, thinking they had seen an angel. For what else could it be? This perfect female form, with a halo of gold, who moved with such grace, and breathed the sweetest air, lifting up the song-birds, the sweet animals harking, all crowding to her. The men. Beauty could do that. That was Lucy.

So they came, those who would not be countenanced by our father, and some who were; for which would not take Lucy over us, enchanted by what they saw? The promise of this beauty facing you across the table, waiting on you around the hearth, beside you in your bed at night, as you… Why care for anything else? No wonder if our suitors carried on down the valley, to join the skulking, open-mouthed pack gathered around Tŷ-gwyn. Hiding behind bushes, lurking behind trees, riding back and fore, leaning against the wall and gate. Worshipping.

It could not be long, before one was chosen, except there were so many to choose. More games needed—'which one shall it be?'

'Am gyd-fydion i gyd-ffatio.' 'Y fi sy'n dirwyn, Pwy sy'n dal?' Candle and pin played.

'Is there any you favour?'—in earnest, now.

Tinker, tailor, soldier, sailor; eeny-meeny; petals pulled from a daisy.

Blue eyes/dark hair/tall, rugged, fair. Lizzie and I thinking of our own leaning, thinking of Owain and Rhun.

But Lucy shook her head and shrugged her shoulders, as if she truly didn't care. Not for any of them. Not then.

My father had not seen Lucy since his return. She was not inclined to come to church, but appeared one day, a lame Mrs Morgan leaning on her arm.

'Bring Lucy home with you,' he said, the morning after.

The words offered lightly into the air, to be caught or missed, without care, his book returned to straight way.

The slipping of a single stitch, in my mother's sewing; her eyes on him, instead.

The smallest of signs unheeded.

And did a black shadow pass by the window? Was there a cock crowing at this untimely hour of the day? Was there any dark omen, near or far?

And if there were, would I have matched its warning to his words?

Why, after all, should he not see Lucy? Had he not been kind to her on her arrival, tending to her needs? When she stayed, in those early days, was she not like a member of his family, for a while, at least? And he—it was him, surely—had arranged her place with Mrs Morgan. A godly, goodly deed.

No reason whatsoever that I should not tell Lucy of his request, no reason at all for Lucy to say 'no'.

And so I brought Lucy home.

She came for tea, first, no more than that, sitting with us at the table, saying little, as was always the case, looking at whoever was speaking to her, him mostly, on and on and on, as if she would be interested in his prattled notions. She looked, she nodded, because that was what Lucy did. And smiled.

'Come again,' he said, as she left. 'Stay longer.'
And so she did.
And when she went, that time, he said he would escort her home. 'On account of all those young rascals who won't leave you alone!' For he had heard of Lucy's admirers, had seen them himself at the church.
And so it went on.

Small signs, straws in the wind, noted, this time, and seeming good, not seeing what could be bad in it. How his visits to the cellar waned, his time spent outside, in its place, working to lose his paunch gained with too much good food and wine, tautening his strung muscles. How he trimmed his beard and ordered new clothes to be made. How I caught him one morning, preening in front of a clear pool, hands on hips, thrusting each side forward, a foolish grin on his face. Pleased, Lizzie and I, for his interest in our marriages had dwindled away.

The talk that came about Lucy, first, was nothing to lift our ears or stiffen our nerves. Rather, it made us smile, bantering words back and forth across the table, adding to them, as we learnt more, embellishing, maybe, thinking it harmless.

'A proper courtship, now, it is said.'
'Which one is it? Do they say?'
'The best looking, no doubt!'
'The best formed!'
'That young farmer, with those dreaming eyes.'
Each of us knowing Lucy cared nothing for such things, wanting nothing more than kindness.
'You must visit. She'll tell you all.'
Was our father there, then? Stood in the doorway, perhaps, or behind the settle, unseen. His brow darkening, his mouth fixed. But if he was, if we had seen, why would we connect his fierce look to our foolish chatter… to Lucy?

Or this—the auguries donning their black shroud, once more. Little by little, tainting. He, still working outside, but not to bronze or prime himself, working, instead, to rid something irking within, jaw tight, body seething. Choosing to scourge the landscape in place of himself.

'He is cutting down trees in the wood,' I told Lizzie, finding him hacking at weeping trunks, saplings and full-formed, heedless, his axe swung high, brought down any which way—no careful eying or hefting. 'Why? They are not the sort for firewood, not rotting or cramped.'

'Harvesting is always done according to season, serving us and the wood. Perhaps he is wanting to bring more land in again. You know how he does that, from time to time. Him, and Uncle Owen. Perhaps our brothers have been coveting even more. Or perhaps he wishes to make an even grander impression on our suitors…'

'… or to sell it, maybe, to put more money in his coffers. But no, there is no rhyme to it… as if he simply wishes to kill…'

More killing, next, easy to foretell when he brings a new greyhound pup home, one already holding the glint of death in its eye, no training needed. He has always done this—hunting is the way of the place, men gathered together with their bluster and bonhomie. Deer. Birds. A brace of rabbits brought home. And I, when a child, looking at flesh floating between roots and leaves—did I say, 'I will not eat this? I have seen this rabbit running through the fields, I have seen its babies in its nest. They will be waiting for their mother's return, and they will die, too?' No. I ate along with the rest, smacking my lips, as they did. And we thanked our father for what he had provided—both our fathers, on earth and in Heaven. That was then.

Yet there was this about him, too—that he had told us the tales of animal spirits, of human kind turned into owl, eagle, boar. And he would speech fulsome praise of beasts, in his verses, scribing their beauty, conjuring the fox's keen eye, its rippling fur.

Now, he and the dog hunted alone, for pleasure, returning from the hills, both proud of what was carried in those jaws.

One day, a hare. My hare, I knew it at once, watched at dawn, when I lingered all night. Golden as the sun rise, knowing as the moon it had gazed at just before. No death-bringer, no druid's diviner, at all. Dew-hopper, wood-cat. Swift as the wind, but not swift enough.

It looked at me, still, dead-eyed.

'For the pot,' my father said, as if he knew.

Soon, the fox was brought—the vixen that came close to me, as I lay in the wood, who talked to me, who allowed me to watch her cubs playing in the clearing, the year before. All rolling sheen gone, her pelt hung dull and matted. No poem, either.

What might be next, I wondered, fearing for the witch in the wood, fearing whip or sword striking with greater ire.

I had never told him of her, but who could say that he did not know, with his spies and all-seeing powers? And rumour came, telling that the witches in the inn had disappeared, the place closed up. Had they simply gone away, seeking pastures new? I hoped, but did not know, just as I hoped the wood witch would be safe. I still kept many hopes and wishes, then.

Black shadows seen again, sleep broken. Peaking between the bedroom drapes, seen rushing from the house, into the woods. Again. Had the wraiths come from the cellar, where Father was once more spending night-fall's hours? Leaving what they had not entered. Were they demons he had conjured—or banished through spell?

For was my father not the Magician of Cynvael? And rumour had it of a new string to his bow—that he had learnt to battle the devil's apprentices... even, maybe, the Dark Lord himself. Was that the reason for his sombre mood, his arcane deeds, taking no more than the cross of a line, a single step away from the light? Rumour spoke of other developments, too—meaning, perhaps, that such skill should be welcomed. For the Devil was abroad amongst us more in that year, come from his dwelling further south, some told.

At first, I ignored such hearsay. Besides, if the Devil was about, would not the Angels be present, too? It was something our father had told us as small children—how they were God's messengers, how they dwelt with us, to fight the demons. 'Look,' he would say, when the sun broke through the clouds over the mountains. 'Look, it is surely an angel, that bright light, come down from heaven, spreading over the land, lifting the darkness, lifting our hearts. And, there, is another. There is one for all of us.' I would tease Lizzie, once we were home, asking her where her angel was. 'I sleep with you. Shouldn't I see your angel? Perched on your shoulder or some such. Hovering above your head...'—which she would then bury beneath the blankets, saying nothing, because what could she say?

Later, growing up, I would look at that light, and see it for the sun, and nothing else. It still lifted the heart, my heart, but it was nature's beauty, and that was more than enough.

And now, when I thought of it, my father himself had made no mention of angels for many a year, as if he, too, had left them behind, and believed in something other. Demons, the Devil, around us, everywhere, so that I could no longer deny.

'I saw him, lurking in the corner of the bridge, waiting to pounce out at me. The shape of a goat, he was. Mourning-black, with horns and cloven hoofs. His eyes, full of fire, stared, as if to send a gushing flame over my body, burning my flesh, my innards to cinders, to blow away in the wind.

'I held my crucifix tight, and said the Lord's prayer over and over again, for 'Fear God and shame the Devil' is what's said. And yes, when I looked again, there was nothing more than a stone, slid down the bank, so I went on my way.'

A black dog, a black cock, a horse, a black pig. A raven (not Arthur, this one!), upon the heights, flying between moorland and marsh, from the slope of the mountain. All these were seen.

'It was Andros, I know it was. Y Fall,' said a stranger, falling against our door one day. 'Unseen, but felt, as he blocked my way—a feeling of terror. Nightmares assail me, and a raging fever, as I fear he has possession of my soul. What can I do to be rid of him? Tell me, pray!'

A dragon-fly his messenger, the caterpillar his cat; a circle of iris his posy, clematis his yarn. The convolvulus that strangled the wild rose his entrails; euphorbia his milk. All these were owned as his. All these trappings were here.

On the mountain, I came across men, women and children sitting among the sheep. 'A white sheep is the one shape he cannot take,' they whispered, as I passed. Black-fleeced corpses littered the scree. A raven, again, waiting. 'Tell your father,' they said.

My father… did they—did all of them—think my father could send the Devil packing, whence he had come? But—this was what I could not comprehend—was he with him, or against. There were always those who made pacts with Satan, near or far. Had he become one of them?

For our barn was full of crows, again—black, squawking, winged creatures. 'Birds,' I told myself. 'Corvid-kin.' Not black-hearted demons Father had garnered, to keep them away from those they might molest. Or… keeping them close, till he wanted to use them for his own ends. Messengers, scaremongers, harbingers. His own purpose, or that of the Devil? Which?

I told Lizzie of their presence, thinking it time, needed. I spoke of the black shadows.
  'Have you heard the talk of Andros about the place?'
  'Did you see the man who came to our door?'
  I saw the blinking of her eyes, the slight jig in her seat. And knew she lied when she said 'no', she was too busy with her books. And knew she felt the fair-weather-foul, but would not own it—nor own that she was kept from the cellar, minding that the seventh child should inherit all his arts.
  And the communion we had known when we were playing at rhamanta, or joined against our matchmaker father dwindled away.
  While Lucy, of course, we did not see, busy as she must be with her new admirer.
  'She must be so happy.'
  'When will they wed, I wonder? We shall help her, of course, make sure it is an occasion to remember, provide her with all her needs.'
  'Be her maids of honour! Darling Lucy!'

More idle chatter between us, after church talk, gossip running ahead of the tale.

The chair, clattered to the floor, the slam of the door. Our father. But had he not burnt his hand, poking at the cinders in the grate, one flying forth and scorching his fingers? Why else should he be angry?

I took to the woods once more. The woods, the river, the mountain. I talked to the trees, instead of Lizzie and Lucy. I lay beneath the Oak, and told it all my fears. It listened carefully, as it always did, nodding its branches around me.

I wrote spells and wishes on the bark of the birch, moon-bright, whether day or night. For birch had the power to make spells and wishes come true. But what was I asking? All was mist, not clear morn. And if I brought the trees to my side, might Father take against them—he who believed he was stronger, believed man to be greater than the magic of the wood? Was he, or the Devil, or both, working against it already, tainting it with their black art?

Deeper, it was always so, its trickster ways showing. How a path might appear in front of you, not noted before. But it is there, no denying. 'An animal, that's all. Made overnight. A troop of badgers, that's all.' You follow, deeper. And, following, you near the heart, away from any feature known. The river, the Oak's grove, the line of the sky above the mountains. All gone. All you see is the bruised line of the path, leading you on... and on, deeper, darker, through thicket of bramble, thorn. Tangled, caught, alone.

No. Because that is when the voices will come. Not the sweet voices of the wind trilling through the leaves, or the gentle mulling of the swaying saplings. There is whispering, yes, but it is of a different kind, snide, as girls gathered together to mock another. You cannot make out the words, but you know the intent. To hurt. Yet you cannot resist moving closer, wanting to share.

But now there is moaning—when you, foolishly, take it for a person, a child, a damsel in distress—someone further down this path you follow, who has travelled before you. And they have fallen, or are trapped by the snares of briar, or bramble and they are crying as they lie there, bleeding, dying, they will die if you do not reach them. So it goes on, and you go on, as the moaning grows more terrible, until it is all around you, and you clasp your hands to your ears, to stop it, but that does nothing. And *you* fall to the ground, then, and *you* will be the one bleeding, wounded, dying…

I knew not to take these paths, but villagers were spoken of, who took short cuts, losing their way. Some, when they returned, stepping out, between the trees, rubbing their eyes, forgot all that had happened, yet were never the same, befuddled, or struck by the night Mare, e'en in day. Some were never to be seen again. A tale of lost children, boy and girl, gone to gather firewood… gone, without a trace.

A story. There was always a tale of lost children, in the wood, on the mountains, this year, last year, every year. I shook it, them, out of my head and kept to the paths, the parts I knew, but knew, besides, there was an awe feeling about the trees, as if they were holding their breath. Waiting. Something I was doing, too.

     rrr,
    River… rive   black, bold, bucking. Afon. Cynfal. The river, too, showing its dark side. Swirl…
    …ling, where it should be calm, placid, sed…dayte. NOISE!!! Noisome, when it should be hussshhed. SShh, listen. To what? What is there, in it, in the rivvaa? Not my river, now. No. His. Whose?
    Or theirs. An impress in the spray, easily seen. A trick of the light. Or. Ghosts. Spirits with long, flowing tresses, that dived and ducked between the eddies. Not the water

sprites, no. There was nothing gentle or playful in these, as they leapt towards the bank, where I stood, enchanted, wanting to coil their snaking bodies about my legs, to pull me into the water, down, down, lost in their folds.

Something other, later, again as I stood, caught. Wraiths, between the weeds, skitting and slithering. 'Fish,' I told myself, 'an unknown kind, travelled up from the sea,' knowing they were not fish, there was no fish of that nature—unnatural, as they were. Eel, then, fish and eel joined in some aberrant coupling, birthing this. No. Or yes, but a human mating, ordained by some greater power—the greatest of the water's lords.

Lord of the torrent, Old Man of the River, who cast his spells upon the stream, changing it to his whim. Playing games, here, with the water, turning it to his bidding, loving the havoc wrought. Old Man, looking down on the flooded bourn, a wide grin spread across his face. Kin to my father, charming mist to his wiles. Kin to my father, growing in height, girth, to subdue his audience in awe.

    'His countenance is fearful, with hair past his shoulders and bristling brows.'
    'His laugh, a rising screech.'
    'Half fish. Or beast. Or both melded as one. Or…'
    I have seen my father like this. I have opened his box of tricks, his dressing-up cupboard, of wigs, hairpieces and false brows. Shaped noses. Of ragged costumes, hair shirts and scaled leggings. Shape-shifting is easy with a few props.
    This cannot be my father, can it? Stealing into the wood, far along the river, to put the fear of… God?... the Devil?... into all those near. Turning wood and river to their dark side—his side, not against. But why?

And can *this* be him? The ceffyl dwr—not that, no, no matter what others. No matter that a clergyman is said to ride on its back, no matter that he is, or was, a clergyman.

See, hear, again, what I had seen before. Saw at the sea, when I visited… ever there. Here, they come and go, but when least expected. No flood, no storm. Hear, for hearing comes first, crashing, pounding, grinding down the rocks, like giant's teeth. Seen, then, galloping, like their namesake, all frenzied motion and force. Notice the one, greater than all, a monstrous steed, with flowing white mane, pennant white tail, its hooves the size of giant's cauldrons.

And I, stood spellbound again, see it rear, half of his body out of the water, turned towards me, looking into my eyes, with his own that were colourless, yet shooting flame.

'The end, now,' I thought. Picturing his rise full out of the water, as he comes just for me, only me, to beat me with his hooves, to bite me with those teeth, to bring the bulk of his huge body down on me.

But no, he turned once more, back among his lesser minions, to carry on down with the flow, looking for other prey.

Afanc… No, not the creature of shining coat and broad tail, not Llostlydan, listed by Hywel the Good; revered by the Druids, but lost, gone. Not that, at all. Instead…

AFANC!!! AAffanc… AFANC!! You do not see the Afanc, the worst of all its kind. Tales told centuries old, tales told to scare, on grandmother's knee. But you have never seen him, you, who swim in the river more than any other; you, who walk its banks, day by day. So—no more than a mythical creature story/story creature, twisted to river's tastes and means.

You will not believe it, you will not fall for it—this once-upon-a-time to keep foolish maiden from handsome youth… a leviathan magicked all-the-better to lure her to his watery lair. The End. For you tell yourself you are not simple enough to fall for such a trick. Simple… or beautiful. Why does Lucy flash into your mind just then? Not mockery, nor envy, surely, you hope.

So what is it that brings her there?

The days, weeks, passed.

We saw less and less of our father, lost in the bowels of the house, or roaming who knew where.

And the omens were gathering like storm clouds, downcast, threatening.

'Have you seen them?' I asked Lizzie, sure she must own them, by now. 'Look, there are doves circling overhead, and doves never signify any good for a place.

'And Mary says she came across a black hog, wandered into the yard, and you know that can only forebode ill.

'The bees have left the house—those that were nesting in the scullery wall.'

I told her all these happenings, and more, all tokens of misery to come.

'These are the notions of the ill-educated, those who know no better.'

'Yet you joined with Lucy and me in the Rhamanta.'

'That was no more than a bit of fun. The studies I have made with Father use scientific methods of deduction, of prognostication. Birds, animals, and the like are no more than superstitious nonsense—good, maybe, for shepherds to tell the weather, but nothing else.'

And, again, she returned to her books. 'I have much to do. Father is giving me much to do.'

'But Father is hardly ever here, or is down in the cellar, where you are not allowed.'

'It is not that, but…'

'But what?'

But she said nothing in return, stamping back to the library, and shutting the door in my face.

And then there were more words about Lucy, brought by my mother, this time, back from a visit to her own family, having called on Mrs Morgan on the way.

'Her sweetheart has abandoned her, Mrs Morgan says. She says she has no idea why, and spends her time crying in the corner, or wandering the woods, and up hill, then down dale, as if she had swallowed some love potion of secret receipt. Donning a willow-cap on her head, searching east, west, north, south, with an apple-seed in her palm. Poor thing… though Mrs Morgan is beginning to fret, on account of her neglecting her duties about the house. Perhaps you should go to her, Mared. You have always been a friend to her. Perhaps you will be able to comfort her, and she will tell you what has happened, and maybe her suitor can be appeased.'

'Will you come, Lizzie?' I asked. 'It will please her to know that you care.'

But no, she would not come, she had too much studying to do.

'Besides, you have always been closer to her. She is more likely to open her heart, if it is just you.'

An excuse to assuage her guilt at her negligence, I thought, but did not say, as I gathered my bits and pieces together, ready for the ride down the valley.

And as I went, was my father watching from the doorway of the barn? Was my father smiling? Or are these yet more detailed imaginings I added to the story, thinking back, not seeing at the time?

A cure for Clefyd y Galon. Heartache…

Take some yarn,
A double thread
Found in your mother's basket,
Or pulled from a loose hanging…
Any yarn will do.

Take your yarn
To a dyn hysbys,
A conjuror.
A shrewd woman or man.
Any such wise learned will do.

Watch as they measure it
On your naked arm
From elbow to middle finger,
One, two, three.
Naming, as they do,
The Holy Trinity.

In the name of the Father,
In the name of the Son,
In the name of the Holy Ghost,
I give my name to thee.

Cut it, knot it, then
Wrap the thread
Around the neck,
From dawn till dusk,
Thrice, again.

Then bury it beneath the ash,
In the name of the Father,
The Son, The Spirit—
All three.

Look and look, time after time,
To find the fate of the lover.
Measure again, in the same way,
To the tip of the middle finger.
If the thread grows short,
There is but little hope.
If it lengthens… maybe.

See Lucy.

See Lucy run. No, not run. See Lucy fly. Flying through the trees, like a bird she cannot name. A hawk with barred trousers, fixing its eye on the centre of nothingness, dipping its wings between. Names escape her, have done, always, beyond country-calling, her grandmother's gabbling. Some time, as la-la-la rhyme. This. 'Take some yarn…'

Hear that, as it runs through her head, a cure for heart-sickness, clefyd-y-galon, slipped in amongst a thousand and one lessons, told on a thousand and one nights, versed around the hearth.

Catch the whisper—A 'secret' passed behind the cupped hand. 'Tell no-one, but you may need it one day.'

And yes, this is that day, long after the old woman has passed.

So she flies, seeking somewhere she thinks she knows, another 'secret', behind bramble hedge, down hidden path. A witch's hovel, herb-strewn; a witch's brew, herb-stewed—what she needs. She thinks.

Feel the pain she feels all through her, wracking her body from head to toes, not only her heart, where it surely belongs. 'Calon…' Her belly curdling, like hag's butter, bile rising through her throat, her mouth, to be retched away.

No more than bile, when there is nothing eaten. No more blood, too frail for her bleeding. Yet there was blood before. Then…

So she flies, because this cannot go on.

Feel her yearning, for her lover's return, so much she wants him back, so much she has done. Picture the memories, inside her head, with each swish of branches, grazing her mind. An image, here, words, there—more words from her grandmother, more of her spells. Telling her to throw her potion into the fire, noon or midnight, either one. 'And your lover's love will come to you again!' But how to get that magic potion, a devils' draught, of quicksilver and dragon's blood? How, first, to find your dragon?

Rewind the story, no flying, then. Her legs weighting her to the earth, her lungs pulling her back, her heart beating her down, as she climbs. Climbing to the highest spot, River followed up, not down, the way she came here turned on its head.

No flying, come to rest, stilling herself, instead. Legs, lungs, heart quelled, to turn this way and that; hand to brow, against the brightest star, to seek what she must get.

'Here,' she thinks. Or 'there?' There, where the coldest wind comes from, there, the warmest; there, where the star rises, or sets? There, in the deepest shadows of the hills… except… there are so many, sun fooled, cloud tricked, shifting up and down, across.

'Here,' she prays, praying for a cleft clawed out, signed 'dragon lives within.' The bones of its prey, littering the scree, blood run down the fissures, rock stained red. Fire, she should see fire, smoke rising from its den, from the flames that flared from its mouth. But… nothing. There is nothing.

And what if she finds it, what then, what could she do—the damsel in the tale? A single blast of its fiery tongues, and that would be her end—her flesh all ate, her bones ash, to add to those not there.

No bones, no dragon, no knight to kill, to thrust his

sword deep into its meat, blood welled and caught in a jar…

… no jar to take home, to dry by the hearth, and grind to a powdery dust.

But pretend—pretend for a moment, that she has her dragon's blood—you must ask 'what can she do?' again. How can she mix it with 'quicksilver', when she does not know what 'quicksilver' means?

Hear the word, chafing inside Lucy's head, stuttering, tumbling. She likes the word, she knows that… and knows how she likes or doesn't like—words, things, people— liked, if there is that warm feeling around her heart.

'Quick.' 'Silver.' Breaking the word up, as some have shown her, when she has looked at them askance.

'Silver', rolling around her tongue. She knows silver, has seen it round your throat and waist, or on the rich ladies in the church. Chains made from it, there. Bright, shiny, pretty—yes, a thing to like.

'Quick', darting through her lips. She knows this, too. Told to be quick about her work. And 'quick' is how she wanted to run, when…

But what is 'quick' of a bright, shiny metal? No, she cannot put the two together. Like so many other pictures in her head.

Feel the weight, now, come inside that head, pressing against her brow; know that a mist draws over her eyes. 'Quicksilver' as far from her as dragon's blood, except…

… this. 'This,' he said, showing a small, blue bottle, on a shelf in a darkened room.

No!

Shaking the thought from her mind, no, no, no.

No quicksilver, no dragon's blood—nothing, to throw into the fire. Let them go, let this go, leave well alone. Gone.

So pull the threads further, to simpler spells, kitchen variety, child-like rhymes.

Hear: 'With this knife this bone I meant to pick:
'With this knife my lover's heart I mean to prick,
'Wishing him neither rest nor sleep,
'Until he comes to me to speak.'
As she sits, scraping meat off blade-bone of lamb, reciting as she works.

Hear it again, 'With this knife… to speak.' And again—'…to speak', till Mrs Morgan pulls knife from hand and her from chair, ''fore lamb and blade fall foul.'

And 'Birch cap, birch cap, thee I send,
'Your way to my love you must wend.
'Bring him back, to soothe my heart.
'For I cannot stand to stay apart.'
Birch twigs woven, in and out, out and in, and scattered all around. Ma Morgan tutting again.

And this, as she wanders about:
'Kernel, kernel of apple tree,
'Tell me where my true love be.
'East, west, north or south?
'Pretty kernel tell the truth,' to no avail.

Or acorns floating in hope of telling marriage.
Or turf boiled hour after hour, to make him start for home.

All these…
Foolishness, all.
Foolishness, after all.

Now fray the yarn back to its start, to Lucy, the wide-eyed child.
Listen to her grandmother, drumming the charms, over and over again.
'This is how it must be, girl.'
'This is what you must do.'

Talking of a time, when she was gone, seeing how it would be. Knowing their need, one day.

And this is Lucy not like others. Moon-struck, sun-touched, changeling, maybe. Whispering that she has gazed on yellow too much, and, yes, she liked the Spring's colours. Whispering, 'Should've been given lavender, to quicken her wits.' So, choosing silence, to hide the words muddled in her head, words that made no sense to most, as they snagged between her lips. 'Most' staring, then, backing away, puzzling the wit-less child. And so, she smiled, instead.

Till… staring, still, man and boy, mouths open, stopped in their tracks; eyes glazed, as if they were spelled.

'Mirror, mirror.' What did they see, that she couldn't—seeing, not knowing, as if that were all?

Mirror, mirror—except there was none, such objects feared, what is behind, coming in front.

Mirror, then, the quiet pool, no wind to ruffle, no trees to jar. A sheltered cwm, a private place, to kneel and look within.

This, her face. See Lucy's face. See it as she saw it, with nothing to measure against, her gran already wizened and bent, her mother and sister long dead. How, then, to tell? Tell what was right, or what was wrong, with the face returning her gaze. 'Me… This is me.' This is Lucy— unmarked, for certain, no small-pox scar, no birthmark, nor mole. Pure, her skin, all round. Fine, the features, within. Perfect beauty, beautiful perfection—but what does Lucy know?

… knowing this—that she had woken one night, crone's breath stealing close, a night Mare with knife in hand. A curved blade, stroking her cheeks, dipping to lips, then grazing from ear to ear. A sinking stomach, telling her to stay, or else the cut would come.

'Nan, Nan?' she whispers, to keep the old woman calm. And breath is drawn back, and knife is slipped away—a dream, maybe, after all. No.

'Forgive me, love. It is a charm, a foolish one, no doubt. Forget, and let it be.'

'Because I'm ugly?' she asks, though it makes no sense—how a gash would make amends.

But her grandmother laughed. 'No, not that!' But what else could it mean?

And she has thought it, still, till coming here, hearing the words rung round—words whispered or said, by the women she knows. 'Beautiful!' 'Such beauty in a girl!'

… till the boys came calling in their droves, her lover's words, licking her ear—'You're so beautiful, cariad, my love.'

He has left her, now. Gone.

She has tried so hard to wish him back, but nothing, nothing has worked, nothing has soothed her pain. And so there is this, in hope.

She flies. See Lucy fly. Flying through the wood, as fast as the fire-fly she caught once-upon-a-time, fast as the fly-by-night, fast as that bird she cannot name. Quick as… silver, if silver runs quick. Flying to find the bramble hedge, to find the witch it holds—if 'witch' she is, for the word was never told. For where else can she go? (Not there, never there, no matter what he can do.)

Hope, with her, for the kindness of the woman, to rid her of this pain.

But… the wood is not what it was. The wood she remembers is no longer here.

Darker, dark, now, though the sun was set on high.

Grey, as gloaming would be, wrapping her round, a blindfold to her eyes.

And the trees, told to be friends, now treat her ill—a branch to catch her hair, another to snag her dress. No flying, now, no bird, barred, hawk, earth-bound, brought down to earth. As bony hands rise up to clutch her legs, her feet, to trip and fell her to the ground.

This—this path she must follow, followed once—it, too, has changed its shape. Or… is not the same. The way it crooks, and slants, plays tricks, taking her back whence she came. For hasn't she passed that hollow beech, once, twice, more? And wasn't River to mountains, but is now behind. Perhaps. Maybe. Or no.

Lean closer, or else don't hear, the whisper begun with her name.

'Lucy.' 'Lucy,' softly said, in purring voice, pleasant enough, at first. 'Lucy, come this way.'

But the track grows blacker, the voice, too, the words no longer sweet. Easily heard, this time round, 'Hurry, you stupid bitch!'

And the bramble pulls downwards, as she was pulled before. And the ground grows soft beneath—leavening, cloying each step down deep, with earth stream fed/bled. A weight from above, a weight all around, pushing her to the floor. And know she has known this, too.

Rain—feel it, heavy enough to rake through the trees, beating twice as it falls from branches and leaves. Her hair, skin, dress soaked, sodden—another weight, weighting on top of the other weight, sucking her into the mud.

She will lie here, for a while, to rest. The mire cushions her, her arms will pillow her head. But the mud is no longer mud, it has turned into a river. It is River, running fast, where ceffyl y dwr rise, rearing their hooves and heads.

Will the Afanc come, as he did before? A shadow, blearing her eyes. Shape turning to hideous monster, ugly and huge, closer, closer, who… She will not remember what he did. Better not to think of anything at all, than to think of what he did. Isn't it what they say of her—that there is nothing in her head?

So better all round grows fainter, still; better it turns to black.

This is what I think has happened to Lucy, near and distant past, pictured inside her head, inside my head. This is what I know—that I find her in the wood, on the way to the witch's house. She lies, tight wound, dormouse-kin, between the sycamore's splaying roots. Fear, mine fearing the worst.

I take her hand, and call her name. 'Lucy.' I see the faintest rise of her breasts, a mirror's cloud, so I know she is not dead.

I have found her, following the trail of breadcrumbs, scattered among Mrs Morgan's chaff. A word, here, a phrase, there, put together to lead this way…

Dawn.

Wood.

Woman.

Find.

… amongst the fret and fuss about her 'charge'.

'Lucy?'

She stirs, begins to speak, not knowing who she speaks to, not knowing anyone is there. A tale of dragon's blood and lost-love spells; of a crone, who taught her such notions. Of a witch who will cure her pain… such pain.

Words fall from her mouth, more words than I have ever heard from her before. As if she cannot stop, as if all the words she hasn't said are freed from inside. But the name of her lover isn't spoken, or where he can be found, or why he left.

'Afanc'—a dread word, whispered… all her words, now, growing awed and hushed. She has seen it, she says. She has seen the monster—he who does unspeakable acts to young maidens. Unspeakable, so that she cannot say them. The words stop then, and turn to cries and moans, as if what she holds inside is too much to bear.

Still she doesn't know me, not knowing when I say, 'It's me, Lucy, Mared. I'm here.'

Her eyes flash from side to side, as if she searches for

someone or something. There is so much fear in them, it fraids me, too.

I pull her up, light as a feather, and lift her onto the pony's back, and lead both back to Mrs. Morgan. She is all soft words, muddled with hard pronouncement.

'Poor mite. Let's get her by the fire. I cannot keep her here like this, mind. I'll make some broth to warm her. What good is she to me, when it is me having to look after her, instead of turn-about? Clean, dry clothes she must have, these are sopping wet. She will catch her... How could I nurse her?'

She cannot stay with Mrs Morgan, even if the old woman wanted her—that much is certain.

Besides, am I not the daughter of the Master of Cynvael? For, whatever I might think of him, there are plenty who will say he has fixed their hurts and soothed their woes.

We put Lucy on the pony again, still in her swoon.

And I tell Mrs Morgan I am sure it won't be long before Lucy is well enough to return to her duties, whilst pressing another purse into her hand.

And so, once more, I bring Lucy home.

My father is the Magician of Cynvael, the Healer, the two criss-crossing, to make something new, to conjure a greater force.

He practises these phenomena to heal the sick, I tell myself. What else would they be for?

He does them now for Lucy, after he has lifted her from my horse, cradling in his arms, whispering, 'Lucy, Lucy,' as he carries her inside.

My mother and Lizzie flap around, bringing water for her to sip, broth, cloths to wipe her brow. But he says, 'No, these are nothing.'

Greater powers are needed. Her true ailment is within. Broth and water are only good for the body, not the soul.

He will employ certain methods to find the cause of her pain, whilst soothing her hurts as he goes. He will need certain of his books, his instruments to do this, and takes her away from us, to his room below.

What? What will he be doing there?

'He will be using the crystal spheres…' Lizzie tells us, to show her knowledge, while the dip of her shoulders tells her pique at staying behind.

… he will pour water over them, and give to Lucy to drink…

'O thou stone of Night and Right, let me dip thee in pure water, to help in this fight…'

… and he will don an amulet, with ribbon, round his neck—the Gospel of St John, inscribed on parchment, enclosed in a bag…

… and he will pass his hand over her, with the power of a magnet, together with the force of his mind…

All these things he will do.

And when she revives, will he do this other—lock her eyes in his, to look inside her head?

He does this, he has done it to me, one of the new skills he learnt on his last journeying. 'It is an ancient technique, practised by the Greeks'—Lizzie, again. He has always done it in some fashion, looking at me straight in the eye, so I find it hard to draw my gaze away. He would talk, in a silky voice, his words clear, as if he were talking to me, only me. Something he did, most, when I was younger, when he was displeased with me. In time, I learnt how to fight it, sending my thoughts away, to another place—the wood, perhaps, or the river, under the water. There— holding my breath, floating free—I could shut my mind, then pull my eyes from his. And laugh. My humours still my own, my secrets still locked safe. Him, displeased, all the more.

'He has done the same with others,' Lizzie has said. Waving a locket in front of their eyes, or a coloured gem, to fracture the light, as they sway.

'He puts them half asleep, then half wakes them, again.'

And they speak, saying truths never said before. What has happened in their lives, what is going on inside.

'To help cure them, nothing else.'

But is it not also said that the soul leaves the body in such a trance? Doesn't that mean death?

Is this another art to play on Lucy? Will she tell him all—all that I heard, as she spoke in her swoon, all that I concocted, besides. All that was closed up tight. Inching it out, thread by thread, until the tale is unravelled, full.

Yet I think of Lucy's eyes, their ceaseless fro-ing, how they came lost beneath her lids. And think, perhaps, he will fail.

And soon, yes, he is there, her in his arms, saying she must go abed. And, yes, broth and water will help for now, until he can try again. But when we wake next morning, her bed is empty and Lucy has gone… how…where?

I will look for her; I will fetch my pony once more, and go straight. I will go down, I will go up, looking all ways as I ride. I will… No. 'No,' he says. He will go alone. For what can *I* do, against demons, fallen angels, and the 'demonic', as this must be. Who else would tell her to leave? Who else would keep her in chains?

So he rides, like a demon himself, and is not gone long, bringing her on the back of his horse, her eyes shut, her rambling quiet. He had found her, easy enough, he tells, in a faint at the side of the road. 'How fortunate that I went so quick and soon!'

There are other cures to be tried.

There will be more spells, of different ilk, a slant this way, a sleight the other, fitter for this particular need. A nudge towards the dark. Or more.

Lizzie preens again, flaunting her knowledge, telling how it may pass.

So here is my father, laying crystal charms around his charge, to protect from evil eye.

And there, he has donned his amulet again, reciting odd words, all the while. 'Rotas, Opera, Tenet, Arepo, Sator,' to send wicked sprites whence they came.

His glinting gem is stilled for this, caught in his ring's claws. Another talisman, to mimic a greater ring, to channel its greater force. Luned's jewel, freeing Owen, son of Urien, from the gate and wall.

And he will read from the Bible, sprinkling holy water, because… isn't he the preacher of Cynvael, too? Because… isn't that what the Evil Minions hate?

All these theatricals he will perform—I think, I assume—painting another picture in my head, adding Lizzie's words, to what I have seen before.

If this is all he does, so be it. Yet, inside me, my stomach sinks and churns, fearing he will do more. Yet what 'more' is, I do not know.

But I am wrong, it seems, because soon, he reappears to say that Lucy sleeps soundly—'a natural sleep at last. She will soon heal, now.'

My mother. My mother, who speaks little, and is always kind. My mother speaks from behind her loom, saying it is time to take Lucy back to Mrs Morgan—something *I* must do. It is strange to hear these words from her—stranger still, the tone in them, as if in command.

'I'm not sure Mrs Morgan will want her,' I suggest.

My mother's reply is harsher, still. 'Give the woman enough money, and she will do anything.' A true observation, perhaps, but unaccustomed from her. Something else I do not understand.

So I took Lucy, still sleeping, back to Mrs Morgan. And yes, the ample supply of coins I brought kept her complaining to no more than a grumble, as we tucked Lucy up, and I kissed her goodbye.

Shame.
Shame, looking back at myself, how I behaved then. Forgetting her for easy thoughts and body's pleasures, as Owain spoke to me, rather than Elin, when we left the church. As he asked me to meet him in the woods, once, twice and more. And my heart did more than skip, when I saw him, near or far. And my body heaved, too, when we lay together beneath the Oak.
Selfish thoughts, to stop me thinking about my friend, and how love had spun her a fraying thread.

'Poor Lucy.' 'Foolish Lucy.' Brushing past my ears, nagging at my mind. Talk that drifted above the river, through the trees, between the houses around us.
'Whore.' 'Slut.' Hammering, then, so I could deny them no longer, letting the words in, letting them toss and turn in my head. The way her dresses flashed her ankles or slipped from her shoulders. The way she fluttered her eyes and flaunted her breasts. The way she always smiled at everyone, including strangers. No different from what all girls do, that I have done. And more. I think of my meetings with Owain, and wonder.

'Afanc' named again, how she enticed him from the river— the foolish girl, become his prey, the tricked girl, who gets the blame. This is what the talk says now—how she had given herself to the beast.
'Mrs Morgan says she shouts it in her sleep.'
Afanc, this monster, that creature. A fiend.
Until… the worst monster of all.

'Have you heard about Lucy?' I say to Lizzie.

'What about Lucy?' she replies.

'That she is possessed by the Devil, they are telling.'

She puts down her book, then.

Lucy is here, again.

She is brought by two men, one on either side of her. There is terror in her eyes, and her body bucks and squirms.

'Mrs Morgan says she cannot cope with her no more. Says it can be nothing but the Devil who has done this to her. Wasn't it talked of all last year, how he was around the place, every which when? Must have caught the poor girl unawares. Shame she didn't carry a stick of rowan with her—that would have kept him aways. Mrs Morgan said the preacher would know what to do.'

So easily returned to his hands…

So, it is not demons now, but their master. He is even visible, residing in her stomach—the rise of it, a throb, a movement.

And my father says he has had dealings with the Devil, and that he has learnt how to fight him. 'How fortunate that is.' (See, how fortune plays its part.)

He will banish it from within, he says. That is all he can do.

'What will he do to her?' I ask Lizzie, but Lizzie, white as a wight, shakes her head.

We will watch, we decide, remembering the small window at the back of the house, looking down at the cellar below. But how to see through grimed panes, and thick drapes pulled close?

Lizzie does not know I know where the key is kept, does not like, when I tell her, but allows what I will do. Slipping there, while Father sups, 'to strengthen for the task ahead.' I open the curtains an inch or two, and swiftly wipe the glass, hoping the skulls won't tell.

'We shall be able to make out something,' I say to Lizzie.

And we do.

She utters these platitudes, Lizzie, her talk pandering to him, as it has always done. How it is for the best, how he knows what he is doing, he is the best at what he does, better than the Reverend Prys (dead, supposed), better than the repute of John Dee (long dead, definitely), better than all the witch-finders who worked for the King (dead, also—the King). That he has always worked for the good, against evil, light against dark, God against the Devil. 'It is to exorcise the Dark Lord. I have read about it. It…' But soon, her pandering stops, her prattling stops (started to calm her nerves, I know). Her breathing stops, and soon, she cannot look, and hides her face in my arm.

Is that what this is? An exorcism?

What Lizzie has read about, what I have heard of, but pushed such talk away?

But what do I see? What do I see, weaving together that talk, with my recollection of that room, with the little I can discern, with…

This…

Not my father, not at first.

Only Lucy.

Lucy, laid out on the table I had spied—body length, as I thought. She lies there, unmoving. 'Good,' I think, glad that she will not feel. Soon, she is severed by shadows, as they dance around the room, a fire-fly here, a tolau, there. Widdershins, pell-mell.

Him, I suppose, though he is yet out of sight—him, fragmenting the candle-flames, as he makes his preparations, gathers what is needed, whatever that may be.

But now they blend, to move together, corner-crouched, a magic trick, dah-dah, to flaunt the skulls that line the walls. Candle-lit, within, spouting flame through the sockets of their eyes, their gaping-mouths. I clutch myself tight, to stall my trembling, then think of Lucy, lying so near. And pray she stays asleep.

And 'Pray,' I beg of Lizzie, who has always had better luck with God and his religion than me. But 'Pray,' I tell myself, regardless, for what else can I do?

Praying more, praying harder, seeing what I now see. A giant's form, drawing close to the table, rearing above Lucy's feet. A figure in black, cloak hung with... what... what is this I see? A heart, a kidney—a tongue? (That one, brought back from foreign fields?—me, being right, after all!). Human organs, desiccated, all, more relics of stolen corpse.

All topped with a mask, a skull of... goat? Some monstrous kind? The Devil's creature. There is nothing else it can be. There is nothing else, with long, curling horns, bent down toward their prey.

'Dear Lord,' I whispered. Dear Lord, please God. Holy Father. Please, please. Yet wasn't this on the Lord's behalf? Wasn't it against His most fearful enemy, the Devil, Satan, the serpent, slunk within?

An exorcism—to drive him away.

And I saw the figure, who must be my father, move closer, and push Lucy's legs apart. And I saw the glint of a blade raised high above, the shadow of its descent.

And we heard Lucy's cries, and could stay no more, running hand in hand. Sisters joined for once.

My mother was sitting by the hearth, looking at the ashes that dwindled there, her sewing left in her lap.

We carried the screams with us, but they were there, already, dashing up the steps, clambering through the floorboards, caught in the air.

'We have to stop it, Mother.'

She turned slowly round, and looked at me, puzzling who I was.

'It is for the best,' she said, echoing Lizzie's words, their meaning turned awry.

'Bone to bone, skin to skin,

'Satan come out, Christ come in,' she murmured, then turned and picked up her work.

We slept fitfully for the hours that remained of the night, together in one bed, as when we were children, holding each other close. But when we came down in the morning, the house was quiet. My mother was still at her place, but whether she had been there all night, we could not tell.

'She is gone,' she said.

Dead, I thought she meant. He had killed her.

But no. 'It went well, your father says. He has taken her back to Mrs Morgan together with Emily, who can both look after her, until she recovers fully, and 'do' for Mrs Morgan, so there will be no complaints. It is for the best.' Those words again.

Whose, or what 'best' did they mean?

'And how can she have 'recovered' from that?' I asked Lizzie, when we were alone again. 'You heard her screams.'

'But if the Devil is gone from her…'

'Is that what you think?'

'I…' Lizzie's speech, stopped in its tracks. Lizzie, lost for words. 'But what else could it be?

Lucy is wandering about the place, people are saying.

Mrs Morgan and Emily cannot keep her abed. She has been seen, walking to and fro along the fence, where her lover was wont to wait.

And she walks across fields, where the sheep bleat, then run, feared by her unseeing gaze.

At night, a white shape floats through the trees, some saying 'ghost', others that it is her. 'That girl, who is struck by the moon.'

Moonstruck, touched in the head, away with the fairies. 'Mad' is what they all mean.

I go into the wood, thinking to visit the witch, wishing Lucy had found her, first. Thinking of herbal brews, slipped down her throat, of hand held, and fears soothed. No need for a man, no need for my father, no need for 'learned' ways.

But the cottage is empty, the witch long gone, all her earthly goods with her. The drying herbs and flowers, the bottles of nature's salves, her crystal stones, her cooking pots and tools—nothing remains. The presence of the Devil in the valley has driven her away.

I go to the Oak, bow my brow to it, then sit below its trembling spread. 'Ask,' a voice in my head tells me, while my heart whispers that I do not want to know.

Yet, in truth, in part, I do.

And I say: 'What happened to Lucy?' the words no more than a murmur beneath my breath, in hope it will not hear.

But the Oak hears everything, the Oak knows everything that happens in its forest, and so it begins to tell.

Lucy has disappeared. No-one has seen her for days. Before, for all her wandering, she would return to Mrs Morgan's to toss and turn until dawn.

But not now. And there are no sightings in the wood, along the river, up to the mountains, or down. Nowhere, near or far.

My father… my father, again, the Master of valley. My father, shouting loud, my father blowing hot and horn, as he musters the men of the commote. They will search for her, because he has commanded it, and because he has plied them with lucre. And he will ride with them, at their head, 'because the girl knows me.'

'Run, Lucy, run,' I tell her… if I could tell her, if she could hear.

'Run.' But how?

If you were to see Blodeuwedd running, would it be like this? Oak reaching a root to trip her, not caring it birthed her, ruled by another, now. Sycamore… ivy-strung… stretching out its threads towards her, to brush her neck—a tender spot, meadow-sweet soft, white—then twine their way around.

Or see the stones in the river grease their heads with weed and bird-slime, to lip her into the water.

Flooded water, (over)flowing flow-er, out of season. A spell. A magician's working. Don't cross here.

See, Lucy running in Blodeuwedd's footsteps. Tell her not to cross where River spates. Tell her to go further up the mountain, to leave it behind, and to spit, if it's after dark. Tell her don't look back, rather than see what is coming, who is coming. Better she doesn't know. Tell her all this. Tell, to help, for she has no help like Blodeuwedd—no maidens holding hands, mewling, pulling, urging, each other on.

Say all this to someone who cannot hear, deafened by the roar of the stream, cowed by fear, by the thoughts rattling inside her head—besides, she is alone, I am not there. And if I were, who am I, but my father's daughter?

Yet husht, hark, Lucy is talking, note her lips' incessant mouthing. So who is she talking to? Herself, her lover, or those she tried to tell once before? The witch, the Oak, the guardian maidens? Her long-dead grandmother? You? Me?

Wait, Lucy, wait a while. The men on horseback are riding to save you. But what will their leader do? He, with the fastest steed, who knows this place, who knows her. He, who has seen her inside.

'Run, Lucy, run faster!' But where is she running to?

I ask the Oak, again, speaking loud and clear this time, but, strange, it does not answer. It shakes its leaves from side to side. Does it not know (but how can that be?) or will it not say? And if that, why?

Will *he* be using his charms of augury? Will *he* know where to go? My father, on his fleet mount, having left all others behind? Will he reach her, first? And what, then, will he do?

I ask the heads beneath the Fall, the maiden-guardians granting me this audience, this favour, 'for Lucy'. But neither can the heads answer my question; or, like the Oak, will not. And they lower their eyes, and the maidens tell they have never done this before.

I wish for the witch to be here, for she would use the mandrake or thorn-apple to find out what is hidden. But she is not.

River tells me. River bringing a story, as it does. Telling parts played—hero/heroine/villain… all.
Girl running through it, splish, splash, like the long-ago before. Gone up towards the mountains, same, too. Words up and down, words ruffling like waves, plashing through me, showing me where to go. I follow…
… up, up, to where River disappears, back into earth, whence it came. River beginning/ending, story, too.
I drink, seeking slake of thirst, spirit's strength, thanking River's spring. I catch my breath, for I have run, too, then look about me. But I see no lonely figure.
I am too late, I fear…
… fear as Blodeuwedd did, as she ran past here. Fear, as Lucy must feel, when she came, too; each, both, reaching the lake, where I now go.

The Lake of the Maidens, this, here, lapping at my feet. This… maybe.

Lucy shouldn't have come here, mistaking the tale. Or… the tale was mistaken, words, names slip-shod. A wrong name given, 'maiden' misshaped from 'handmaids' who waited on the flower queen, in her marriage bed. Not virgins, at all. Perhaps.

Imagine them, after all, trapped in their castles, ruled by guards, knights, squires—menservants, no doubt. What good is a door, before a lusting man? What good are closeted, cosseted damsels against a man's brute force?

See them running, as you saw Blodeuwedd.
A different gait, them, not carved from broom. Better? Worse? Who might tell, or compare?

Still they trip on the roots, and get caught by ivy's bind. Bare feet and fairy-shoes are no good against the magicked wood—or soldier's boots and wrath.
Still they try.
Try and try, to reach as far as here, and reached, yes, then looked behind.
And fell, drowning.

The lake will not give Lucy what she wants, that is my hope. But still there is no sight of her. I walk one way, run another. I call her name, again and again. 'Lucy'. I hear it back, echoed from the mountain lee, then hear it pebble-skimming across the water. But there is no answer.
And I know what I must do.
I must become a fish, blood turned cold, to swim in cold mountain lake, where water never warms.
I must hold my breath tight, my lungs wracked, taking

me down, down, from one side to the other. Around and around, eddying the water, I shall go, as I look for Lucy.

So, down, down, I do go, water filling over, above me, letting me in. My baptism again. Again, and ever since, it has always been. Feeling the press of it upon me—my skin, my flesh, my lungs at first, inside, outside, against each other, pushing. Yet River has taught me well, River has shown me what to do, storing my breath safe, like some precious thing. And River moved, brushing, rushing, pulling this way and that, while the lake is still, a basin of water. Easier.

Easier, easing, swimming, splayed hands spreading the weeds, to glimpse what lies within, what they may hide. Silver fish, or curious creatures of the mountain llyn— wanting to see no more than should be.

I paddle my feet as one, as if I have no feet, just as the seals and mermaids do, the selkies do, undulating me, them, propelling on towards the deeper centre.

There are stones here, memory returning them to me, stones shaped into ruined huts from long ago. I recognize them, seen again, coaxing them into truth. A village, once-upon-a-time, where folk dwelt happily. Mermaids, selkies, or a realm of the fairies. The Queen of them, returned to her domain, after her mortal marrying. Such wonders are known. Or… was there no water? Did land sink, or flud rise, drowning a village of men? Such misfortune as that is also known. They, too, are in my mind, seen before, their shadows in and out of the houses—going about their daily tasks, it is pleasant to imagine. Perhaps the spirits of the virgins have joined with them, finding another life in their watery grave. Not so hard, after all.

Will Lucy find a home with them in time? If Lucy is here? I do not want Lucy to be here, but…

They say the body of a drowned man floats face down, while a woman looks to the sky. It is not true. Or… it is not true for Lucy—I do not see her face, and I am glad. It is her hair I notice, first. Yes, there is weed that grows fine as spun silk, drawn out from the chinks and crannies. But there is none of this colour, of her colour—golden wheat, caught in the morning sun.

She cannot have been here long. Only a few worn patches daub her skull, where the fish have nibbled away. Like birds gathering for their nests. Do fish nest, too? They will come for the rest of her soon. Like birds, in that, also. Already settled on her eyes, perhaps, orbs of the bluest summer sea. I will not look. I will not move her. I do not want to see!

And she cannot have been here long, because her body has not swollen, as bodies do under the water. It is still in its perfect form, no more than a bite-size taken, here and there.

If I had come sooner… if I had known sooner… if I had…

I reach my hand out, thinking to touch her in final farewell, but I cannot, I cannot. And I must leave now, I must return to the surface, my time here, done. There, perhaps, I can say 'goodbye'.

The water has finally rid the Devil from Lucy. Is that what she thought? Is that why she walked into the lake, and kept on walking, until she was beneath it—fully beneath, so the water would rest above—so that, no matter if the Evil One could walk on water, as some said it, they would still be parted? The Devil would be finally gone.

But what Devil was she thinking of, as the water stopped her breath, as she sunk to the bottom, as her life flowed away?

I will not go home this night. I walk back down the mountain, follow the river, then into the heart of the wood. I lie down beneath the Oak, where I pray for Lucy's soul.

The soul hovers between earth and moon, it is told. I look for it, but see nothing. I climb the tree, as high as I can, until there is emptiness between me, on this earth—just—and the bright disc in the sky. But still nothing.

Other pronouncements are offered, too, about heaven, about hell—the underworld, reached by crossing the Pool of Dread and dead bones, then in to the gaping mouth of the Abyss. Should I look down, not up? Should I visit the ash tree and wonder if she is trapped, there? But what am I looking for? For what does a soul look like? Any soul? What does Lucy's soul look like? And what if she cannot have one, because she has sinned, no bargain made? Would she prefer, besides, to return as a ghost (as was said of her, before), a wraith in female form, who runs through the wood, along the river, Blodeuwedd, again? A ghost who haunts those who wronged her.

I fear she is neither. I fear she is no more than a body in the lake, getting bigger and smaller all at once, as her figure swells with the water, while the fish eat her flesh away.

And I see her corrupting body float in front of my eyes, again. And wonder if it will ever leave me.

This, though… the sky darkening, the stars waking, strung out between earth and moon. The stars, full of their stories, sent down. I have lain in the wood, watching, listening, searching for the dwellers. The circles of Dôn and Sidi. Arthur's Harp, Plough-tail, and Yard. The cauldron of Ceridwen, the chair of Eiddionydd. The nervy Tŵr Tewdws. Gwydion is there—Caer Gwydion, with its fiery pathway leading down to earth. His sister, Arianrhod—I have seen, I can see, the four points of her crown, bright gems. She is there, taken from her island in the sea to the north, to rule in the sky at night. Far, far, away, time-jumping, distance-hopping, two places at once, her brother not the only shape-shifter.

As a child, when I said I loved the stars, when I spoke

of their beauty, their stories, my father laughed. He gave them Latin names, Via Lactea, Pleiades; measured positions, cited their value in navigation—Lizzie scribing in her little book, all the while. Another subject to study, not to stare at, and love. Later, he talked of them in different ways, with different names, how each of us matched certain of them, ruling our affairs. Predicting the path of our lives. 'Astrology', he called it. He gave them symbols, kept secret from the unknowing, as if in the dark.

But the stars shine through, shine on everyone. They are there for all of us.

They are here, above me, and I want to think that Lucy is up there, as beautiful as any of them. And that she will stay there, burning brightly, and be happy, for all time. But I remember her body in the lake once more, and I cannot. All is darkness, there.

The men are gathering, for another day's search. I see them, as I make my way back home. I watch my father, at their front, as before, commanding, cajoling and I watch them, as they head downstream, mistaking where she lies. And I let them carry on. I do not tell them where they can find her, I let them—him—carry on. Perhaps Lucy will appear nine days after her death, and they will see her then, and they will know she is dead. I hope *he* will see her, I hope *he* will know everything he has done.

I do not, I will not forgive him for Lucy.

I must grow, myself, now. I must slough my skin, and take another form, do what he does, to defeat him. Because that it what I am going to do.

Today I will be a bird.
Bird. Eagle.

Bird. Crow.

Bird. Lark.

Bird. Owl.

Any of these, all of these, so that I can fly to the top of the mountains, I can see at night, I can go amongst the fleeting shadows. So that I can learn all I need to learn about the dark arts.

Today, I will be a fish. No, not a fish! For I do not like to think of what the fish are doing to Lucy. So no fish for me. I will, instead, be some other water creature, swimming in the river, to be as fluid as the stream. An otter, perhaps, snaking, slipping, snatching those fish, feeding my revenge on them, letting it grow with the breath in my lungs. A mighty thing. Coursing the river from start to end, till nothing is hidden. All is shown.

Today, I will be a hare. *My* hare returned, I would like it to be, able to run across the fields, to hide beneath the tussocks, to twitch my ears, and listen. Telling who is where, when. The hare will read the land, as the otter reads the river—both revealed. And the hare is the witch's friend, or the witch herself, enchanted. But no… I do not have that power. Yet.

I become the eagle, again. The King of the Birds, whirling the air above the mountains, flying the highest of all the birds, except the wren. High, high, looking low, low, searching for the wood witch to help my task. The highest peaks, the sea, the lowlands and back again, are no more than a flap of my wings for me.

But the witch is nowhere to be seen, wherever I go. She is the one who has sharpened her wings and flown.

Today, I will be… nothing. A creature unseen, as I gather fern-seed, and become invisible. But no, that does not happen. I do not have such skill.

The heads teach me many lessons, the maidens guiding, as ever, in the asking, helping me understand what is said. I write my needs on a fragment of paper, scroll it tight, and offer it to them. A root in their mouths. They want other sustenance, too. Bread, mead, coins. I bring those, and lay them at their feet. The maidens thank me with smiles and nods, the heads thank me with their knowledge.

The wood provides.

I make a garter from the green bark of the rowan, and wear it at all times. It will protect me—from conjurors, sorcerers, wizards. But the Devil—that isn't told. Still, I carry a stick from it and wear a girdle of its berries, whenever I can. I am well-protected, am I not, with these and my wishing-cap of hazel leaves, gathered at midnight at full moon—all done, as is required? A memory—Lizzie and I donning our caps, when we were girls, wishing for all kinds of nonsense. There is only one thing I wish for, now.

Still, there are signs I pray for, in the way I pray… asking of another god… a goddess, I like to think. True, I could pray in the church's way, repeating Psalm CIX every night and morning for a year. But I do not want to wait a year, and I no longer trust those ways.

Instead: 'Let white creatures appear here.' The crow, the dog, the fox, the hare—all, if they appear in their colourless form bode ill. The barn-owl on the roof! The cry of the screech owl! I want him to hear! The Deryn Corph, crying, 'Come, come.'

I beg the geese, and hens, and ducks to leave, and for the bees and blue-bottles to come in, and the cricket to desert our hearth.

'Has the church clock failed to strike?' I ask Lizzie one day, as we enter the churchyard. She looks at me strangely, but says nothing, and is still silent when I pluck a flower from a grave as we pass by.

Days, weeks, pass of this, the search for Lucy given up, deciding she has gone elsewhere, most forgetting her soon enough. But I do not, and keep on with my task.

And what does my father think about her? Does he still search, by himself, unknown to all? Or does he hope she has gone, beyond reach in one form or other… beyond ken and telling—which does he do? I look at him, and wonder, and test new spells.

And yes, at last, he is waning. Helped by all these signs and charms, I have managed this. He has taken to his bed with this ailment, and that pain, and some strange malady, which cannot be divined.

'It is as if he has been cursed,' says Lizzie. And I smile.

We sit by his bed, I, in silence, while Lizzie coughs and tuts, and says 'Father,' time and again, knowing the slightest of noises will help him recover, as is said. It is as if we are in some kind of competition, me, to make him die, her, to keep him alive.

Mother moves in and out, puts a drink to his lips, and mops his brow. What does Mother think? What has she ever thought? We do not know.

Lizzie reads to him, from his own books, and he fixes his eyes on her, not on Mother or me, but her, as she reads from his sermons, repeats his recipes of healing, his magic spells. 'You have done such good, Father. You must recover, so that you can do more!' From time to time, he stretches out a shaking finger, to point at some particular reference in a particular book. Then Lizzie will fuss and do as is commanded—make a potion, perform a ritual—whatever might make him well. But still with no avail.

More days go by, more weeks. His cheeks sink before our

eyes. His hair straggles into wisps that shed themselves onto his pillows. His skin yellows and thins. But still he does not die.

He does not want to die, a man like this never does, thinking too much of themselves, however ill they become. They will fight and fight and fight. He will fight and fight and fight. I perceive it all now—how the black arts he returned with on his last journey were the kind to foil death; how the charms of a beautiful young girl were craved, in order for him to feel alive—taking the years away, restoring his vigour, feeding his flesh. But Lucy did not want him, she loved her lusty young man. And so…

I turn to my task again.

When Lizzie goes from the room, as even she must from time to time, I take the flesh of his arms between my fingers and squeeze.

'Look,' I say, on Lizzie's return, 'black and blue marks, which can only mean one thing.'

Outside, I dig over a new flower bed, just below his open window. 'Can you smell freshly-turned earth, Liz? I fear it cannot be long.'

I rap and tap and scrape my chair across the floor, a true clacket. 'The Tolaeth… it must be the Tolaeth, Lizzie, that noise. And I have heard the Cyhiraeth, too, such a doleful cry, a shriek, even, leading from here to the churchyard. And I saw—I am sure I saw—the Canwyll Corph, here, here, in this very room. You know what that means! Poor Father.'

But Lizzie works the other way, digging deeper into his books, for the strongest of his spells. And she, after all, is the seventh daughter of the seventh son, or so it is alleged, chosen to be the inheritor of his powers—a magician in her own right, should she choose to be.

True, the jealous grandmothers say all a seventh child can do is heal a rash, yet, in truth, he and she have more knowledge than me. What am I, after all, but a daughter of the river, the wood, who has learnt from the ancient ways? What is that against the Devil?

This is the mood upon me, when I see his breath grow stronger, or as Lizzie waves her hand over him, as she cites from his books another spell of healing. And another.

This: a cure for ague, when the fever is upon him.

I have watched her leave the house on slippered feet, creeping towards the hollow willow that stands in the corner. I have watched her return without looking around or speaking a word. I know what she will have done, breathing into the willow's empty bole, then stopping the opening straight way. Wishing, now, I had cut the tree down…

This: when he holds his hand to his head, and wrinkles his eyes in pain. She fills a bowl with melted tallow, another with cold water, and lowers his brow within—just as he would do to the farm urchins.

This, this and this. The arcane knowledge of the seventh child, together with his 'scientific' doctoring she finds in his books. The carefully labelled phials in his study, the leeches to be administered for bleeding, the hearing-trumpet for listening to his heart and breathing.

What hope do I have against these twin assaults? What chance do I get, with Lizzie unminded to leave him, brushing my own simple magic under the bed?

What can I do? I cannot do this on my own. But who can I call on to aid?

My mother? Yes, my mother is another from a place of legend, a family of the wise, of dyn hysbys and lore-ful grandmothers. But my mother does not have these skills, beyond her knowledge of flowers and herbs—useful enough in their way, but no good for summoning the end.

Besides… what does my mother think of her husband's dying? Still I do not know.

I watch, as she brings his broth, and fends his needs, but soon she goes. And find her, back at her spinning, her harp, her garden, happy to leave Lizzie stayed.

And she has no tears shed over him, or protestations or prayers. No 'dear Lord, please make my beloved well again. Please do not let him die!' No desperate pleas to Liz to cure him, or frantic supplications sent to others—brother Owen, or Reverend whichever—to come quickly and help. But my mother has never been one to tear her hair and rend her clothes, which does not mean she does not feel inside. 'Does she love my father?' I wonder now, as I have wondered before. Yes, or no—which? And I see myself surprised, when she wanted Lucy gone, after Father's first 'healing'. And a flinch in my memory tells me it was Mother who arranged Lucy's situation with Mrs Morgan, after her first stay.

What did she know, from all that time ago? What did she know of all happening since? Everything? Nothing? Perhaps she would not care if he died... or perhaps she would care too much.

But... I cannot know for certain. And it does not mean she would help me, whichever way. Besides, what can she do?

And still the days go by, the weeks, and my father, I fear, begins to rally. This cannot be allowed to happen—that he grows well again, and his machinations with the Devil continue. And he escapes any punishment for what he had done to Lucy.

I search for the witch again, to no avail. I look for the 'sister' witches, in spite of their limitations, but yes, the rumour is true, the inn is deserted, they are nowhere to be found. I work through my spells again, and more. I need more.

I return to the wood, and do reverence to the Oak. Might it release the wood-nymphs to help me in my task? I picture them gathering from laurel, ash and fellow oaks, coming together at the Ford, where they will meet the water-sprites—for I will ask the river to free them, too. So many creatures of enchantment, escaped from bark and flow, all ready to give me their aid! I see them—what? They cannot move beyond their enchanted domain—and if they could, what then? They are no more than diaphanous spirits, who are used to hiding and frittering. All faint and insubstantial. They have nothing to do with Death, in all its Dark forms, unless it be of tree or stream. They will have nothing to do with my father's ending.

Gwydion. The true magician, the one my father has always mimicked, but never equalled—nor come near. Is there some way I can summon his power, to channel it for my own needs? Perhaps he will order the trees to battle, as he did once before—so much better than wisps of dryads. Gwydion, who vanquished Pryderi, with courage and strength, magic and spells. He, who could marshal his arts to thwart all who stood against him. He… Yet, there is this, also, about Gwydion— how he countenanced the rape of Goewin by his brother, Gilfaethwy; more, how he pulled the strings of all his puppets to let it happen, killing multitudes of Welshmen along the way. How he humiliated Arianrhod, his sister and, some tales say, lay with her against her will—telling that Lleu was not his nephew, but his son.

It comes to me, now, that Gwydion is not the hero I thought him to be—not for woman—kin, or kind. It comes to me that I have been wrong all these years to kneel before his greatness, to see him through gilded eyes.

Instead, I see him and my father, merging as one, rising up to their utmost stature, then thrusting down on a cowering maid beneath. Gwydion, god no more.

He will no longer hold me under his spell.

But is there no-one to replace him in my prayers?

Arianrhod. His sister—that sister, lain with, maybe. She has powers, too—of a different nature, but not without their use. The weaver of time and fate; mother moon; free spirit. Woman. There are skills I could learn from her, if she would grant me my wishes—how to pull this thread, and cut that one, and join those two, to tie up loose ends. But it is at the waning of the month, and the skies are clouded, as if they are part of this nightshade upon us. She is hidden from me, so how can I ask, how can I absorb her light and power? No sister-meet, after all.

And all the while, that other sister, *my* sister, Lizzie, carries on watching over him, whispering her words of encouragement, her prayers, to him and to the Lord, father and Father. Her hand in his, a beatific smile on her lips, willing her strength into him. 'Please, Father, Father, please!'

This… until I tell her about Lucy.

'I know what happened to Lucy.'

She knows. Somewhere deep in the heart of her, she knows—has known, perhaps, as long as I.

There is no questioning. The answers are formed in my head, wait on my tongue, to leap forth, with no need… sent back whence they came.

… As there is no need for me to take her down to his cellar, where I have been many times since he took to his bed. But I do.

I show her the blood on the table, where Lucy lay, how it spatters the floor and walls. I show her the costume he wore that night, pushed into a trunk against the wall—the blood on that, too.

And she understands more than I do. She runs her foot over the symbols that mark the floor, her face curdling at their meaning. She picks up the bottles and jars that line the shelves, and knows from their labels what they contain. She turns over white rocks and red, a wax seal, a round, black 'mirror'. Her eyes linger on the charts adorning the walls.

'Alchemy, as I said before. But not the kind I thought it must be, that I hoped for. It is not to make new medicines, nor even to turn metal into gold—which, though grasping, is not wicked. It is…'

It is as I thought—the desire for immortality, or, at the least, to be young again. Rejuvenation, the perfection of the body, not the soul. For Lucy.

'He has been searching for the Elixir of Life, the Philosopher's Stone. The Magnum Opus has consumed him, with nothing else mattering. And he has turned to the Occult and Supernatural to succeed. Or… they have turned to him, reaching him through his scrying, his divination—these objects. Yet he claimed it was Lucy who was possessed.'

'There is this, as well,' I tell her. It is a journal I have found in a secret drawer, without need of hiding from me—I do not understand the words, beyond the days and dates noted. I know it is not Latin, nor one of his other foreign languages. But, beyond that, I can decipher… nothing.

'Code,' Lizzie says, ruffling the pages, her finger trailing a word, a phrase, a sentence, here and there. 'His 'Almanac' in code. But I can read it.'

And she does, sitting in the corner of his room, for she is not inclined to draw near him anymore.

We are as one, now. Working to the same end. But the ways she works are puzzles to me.

This is a puzzle:

'28, 35, 2, 7 = 72
   '6, 3, 32, 31 = 72
   '34, 29, 8, 1 = 72
   '4, 5, 30, 33 = 72,' I find her chanting, one day.

'Notice, Mared, how they total seventy-two, whichever way you add.'

I do not notice. Numbers have never been important to me, no matter how my father tried to teach me, or how the wood witch chanted three times, or seven times or nine times, 'for luck,' she would say. And three is for the Trinity, Bible and witchery muddling again. I do not notice, I do not understand.

'Never mind,' Lizzie says, seeing my shrug, the fog over my eyes, 'but write them in a square, with his name under it. Fold it, twice, and twice again and place it in a bag, to wear around your neck. It will render him powerless against our stratagems.' I decide numbers have a value, after all.

Soon, this, perhaps, or that   another of her ploys—or the omens I fabricate around the house, in his room, near his bed, outside his window, and whisper their presence to him, work their 'magic' and he weakens once more, until his pulse falters, his heart slows, his senses leave him. But not his voice.

He talks, now, he talks of Lucy. If we had not known before, we would know, now, what he had done. All of it, and more.

Mother stays away, as if aware of what is happening, but does not want to allow it. Perhaps she has heard it all before, in dreams, as they lay together. We let her be. It has come to us that she will not mind what we are planning.

But still he does not die.

'A pillow.

'Poison in his cup.'

'Plain murder,' Lizzie protests. 'Not that. It must be some kind of magicking, his end befitting his life. And to make the right story.'

'But what?'

She is going through his books, again—volumes we found in the cellar, that she has never seen or read.

'There is much I have never known, much I do not like. But there is also plenty that may help us. Strange, Mared, but also somewhat satisfying, if I should find the answer here.'

And she does.

And, 'How long can you hold your breath under water, Mared?' she asks.

This is what we must do…

I must be the otter, again. We must go to the lake by the bridge of the black ford, Llyn Pont Rhyddu, wherever that may be, she must… I must…

But first… 'I cannot let them all go,' Lizzie tells me. 'For all the bad he has done, there is much good in them, from before. Astronomical lore, medicinal virtues, astrological calculations, second to none in the world!'

She is copying pages, paragraphs, chapters, out of his books. She stays up at nights, her eyes straining in the candle-light. I fetch them to and fro for her, from his library, the cellar, huffing and puffing. The weight of so many words! *His* words. These are *his* books, the books of his doings and learning. These are the ones that are needed for our task. And once Lizzie has finished her scribbling, we can begin.

We go, the two of us slipping out early, before sun's awakening. For our way is long, we have discovered, from a map found amongst his papers, marking its course. His books are strapped to one merlyn while I mount the other and Lizzie walks. I cannot be weary, when we arrive. I am gathering my strength, my breath. I ride carefully, my body poised.

We are going north—further than we have ever been—through lonely peaks known only from stories—where the evil witches are said to roam, where the Brenin Llwyd creeps through the ravines, waiting to capture the unwary.

The day is close to half-gone, when we near the lake, crossing the stream by bridge and ford. A barren place, deserted. Good. We do not want any witnesses here.

At the water's edge, I ask Lizzie if she is ready, half-afraid she will change her mind, though she has been staunch so far in all this.

She nods. 'Go,' she says.

I kiss her swiftly, turn, hesitate for a heart-beat, then walk into the unwelcoming water, until it is deep enough to dive.

It is cold, colder than the Lake of Virgins—though both are open to the mountain air, this is higher, cloaked in cloud, shadowed by Eryri's tall peaks.

It is as dark as its name. 'How will I be able to see?' I wonder. I cannot raise my head, that is not permitted. It is only my arms that must break the surface. But where? And how long will Lizzie be?

The water presses around me, as if it has a power of its own. What if the water works for my father, not me? What if it knows what we intend, and will use its power to stop us? Yet the Devil does not like the water.

'Hurry, Lizzie,' I think, feeling the pounding in my ears, fearing the bursting of my heart and lungs. This is not my river! This is something of a different ilk, an older age.

'Where? Where?'

I twist around, pushing my body straight, my feet toward the bottom, paddling away. I think of the otter, the seal, all water's creatures, how they move, how they live. I swim further, then back. I turn my head this way and that, but still I cannot see. The water is dulled with weed and shadow. This will not work. Yet Lizzie said it was written in the books, that it is the only way.

And then… a shaft of light breaks through the darkness. Later, Lizzie will tell me it was the same above the water… how the sun came out between the clouds, the tops of the mountains seemed to part—'a miracle, surely!'—to let a single beam shine down onto the surface.

There, that would be where I must throw the books, I knew.

There, that would be where I would raise my hands, my arms, catching them in the air, then bringing them down into the deep, down, down, as far as I could go, where I let them free, feeling them sink further, picturing the pages dissolve into nothingness, the covers swollen, then rotted, his words—the words that spewed from his mouth, to ferment on this parchment, the words that ruled us all, fooled us all—eaten by the fish. Like Lucy. Gone, forever.

I rush for the surface, knowing that to stay a moment longer would mean an end like the books, like Lucy in her distant lake.

Air. Air, after water. Air, that I have lived in, no matter that I was birthed in the other. I let my mouth, my throat, my lungs, my stomach, taste it, swallow it, revel in it. It plays around me, coming through the mountain passes, which funnel it, and send it straight to me. Air, breath, I breathe. I toss my head, shaking the water from my hair, my eyes, my all. The gloaming before my eyes lifts.

Lizzie is sitting on the bank. I swim, then walk towards her.

'It is done,' she says.

'How do you know?'

She looks at me. I see the confusion on her face, and remember how much she loved him, once.

'I just do.'

And yes, when we get home, my father—our father—is dead.

My father is the magician of Cynvael, the master of all he surveys. My father is a soldier, tall and strong, hale and hearty, my father is…

My father is… a man.

My mother has already washed him. 'He died as the clock struck midday,' she says.

Lizzie and I look down at him, as he lies there in no more than a cloth across his loins. This is my father…

… a man of middling height, worn thin. It is as I thought, all his bulk was an illusion, smoke and mirrors. But his bones, the long bones of his arms and legs are visible above his flesh—the flesh, wan, sap-sucked like the peeled birch. The flesh, what is left, hangs from his bones. And his face—the face that has commanded so much in its time. It has sunken in on itself, cowering away from his mouth, his eyes, down into a scrag of nothing more than furrowed skin.

The mouth, venting so many words—in English, Welsh, French, Hollandish, words of magic, words of the Lord, poetry, learning… hate, the Devil. So many words that it cannot be stopped and opens still.

'It is the gases leaving the body,' Lizzie whispers. 'Nothing else.'

It is hard not to feel pity for this wasted form.

Then I see his hands, and think of what they have done, of the knife they held above Lucy, in Lucy, of what they wrenched from her insides. Of them pushing Lucy to the ground by the river, of them holding her down as he… I cannot see beneath the cloth. I cannot see what he forced into Lucy. I imagine it shrivelled to no more than a dried-up grub-worm, a slug beneath a stone.

There is no pity when I think of all this.

And no. *No!* I will not have it, that this is the Devil's work, that the Devil is to blame. It is man—this man, ruled by his own self, his wants, his needs—who did what he did.

It is said if you allow your tears to fall on the dead, they will have no rest. I do not want him to rest. I lean over him, think of Lucy, and I weep.

Later, I ask Lizzie which of us killed him?

Lizzie threw the books, but it was my hands that rose from the water and caught them. Or did he kill himself, because it was *his* instruction that we followed?

And was it truth that Lizzie destroyed his works, when her scribing saved his most valued texts? It is hard to say, harder to make sense of.

'Both of us,' Lizzie replies. 'Let us leave it at that. The two of us, together. Now, let it be.'

But how to let it be, when there are people come calling, to pay their respects, but never without their questioning? My mother lets it be, does not ask where we were that day, does not ask why Lizzie does not weep and wail and tear out her hair and go into perpetual mourning, as Lizzie surely would. She carries on at her music and garden and spinning, in between making the funeral arrangements, in between feeding the visitors… so many. The Reverend, brother Owen, the farmers of the district, those he rode the hunt with, his congregation from earlier days, when he preached from the stone in the river, others, from further away, whom we do not recognise, yet by their whispering and sly eyes we take to be his fellow spies. And our brothers, his sons, gathering now, to eye him and the house they will inherit—all asking: 'What happened? How could a man of such great power die?'

For, after all, my father was the magician of Cynvael. My father was the master of Cynvael. My father was the preacher of Cynvael. He was a soldier, strong and brave, a friend to kings and queens. A miraculous shape-shifter of nonpareil, an arch-alchemist of himself and the stories— that was where his true skill lay.

And where he lives shape-shifts, by his doing or older ways, together with time playing games, and history chopping and changing. And… *stories*, more than anything else. Think of the witches, remember the conjuror's tricks, Gronw's stone… Lucy… A blink of an eye, a palming of hand, a slip of the stitch or pen, a word writ back to front. You need little else.

So… that is what we do.

We turn the tale, make it into one fitting for such a magician, a fitting end to such a life.

This is what we say:

He is ill—so ill—and wants to die, but wants to take the secrets of his art with him. He asks his daughter, the seventh child, of the seventh, of the seventh etcetera, to throw his books of lore and medicine into the Black Pool. The daughter much desired to preserve the books, being a healer herself, and knowing them to contain calculations second to none in the world. Still, she went to the pool, carrying the precious volumes, but could not, at first, make herself throw them in. Yet she loved her father, and remembered he had told her he could not die in peace, until the books were gone. So she carried out his wish. And, in a beam of light, as the volumes reached the surface, an ethereal hand rose up from beneath, grasped the books and drew them down into the deep, leaving Huw Llwyd to pass peacefully away.

A nice tale.

Our story. I see it further in, from the future—how they will love the hands of a lady in the lake, for they like all such other-worldly beings and, furthermore, they can liken it to Arthur's myth. And they will add and take away, to suit. They will add two tries/lies, so that the daughter visits thrice—always favouring the number three. They will say there is no death certificate and no grave, and so, maybe, Huw Llwyd never died. That he lives still—ah, they love that one, and bandy it about, in hushed tones—or has gone to another body, another human or another creature, maybe. Resurrection—always so welcome, be it by God or magic… whichever they prefer.

Or… he has died, yes, but oh, the wondrous journey of his soul! He is a shooting star, moving between sun and moon. He is in the fleeting clouds, he is in the rainbow, the leaping stag, the eye of the storm. He is everywhere, about us all!

And it will be written down, Lizzie is writing it down, as she has written so much down. It is her new form of scribbling. 'I am recording what has happened,' she smirks. 'It is important that the truth be committed to paper,' whilst knowing there is no such thing as 'truth'. Stories in black on white can be scripted according to the scribe, corrupted by whomsoever is choosing the words, just as easily as the spoken word is lost in the wind. To be warped, again, by he, or she, who reads, into whatever cloth they want.

Lizzie… who carries on his work—another form of resurrection. But only the best of it, of that I am sure— tending to the sick, preaching to soothe troubled souls, seeking knowledge for the good, nothing more. She stays within the valley, in a house provided by our brothers for her and our mother. It is a simple dwelling, together with a garden, where my mother grows the plants for Lizzie's needs. It is all they want. And she goes no further— travelling between the farms and the cottages, the poor folk her flock. No fur-lined robes, no magic tricks, no standing on a pillar of rock in the middle of a stream—just her.

And me…?

River…

'A-fon', 'Cyn-vael'. Hear it.
    Hear the river, hear the word.

Say it—rivvaaa. Roll it round your tongue, rolling like the…

River. *My* river. Lullaby, nag. Friend, foe. Shape-shifter.

Shifting flud, bourn; ceffyl y dwr, millpond. Spit, splash, plash, rattles down the mountain, snakes, rushes, dawdles, as it drags its arms behind.

Waters broke, birthed me, my mother said. *Here. There*—the river birthed me, birthed this place. Coming down from the mountain, scritching bit by bit, the rock, the earth. Eating it, you could say.

'Put your hands, scrunched to your ears.' Still you'll hear it. Not the blood in your veins, the trickster shell, spat from the sea, fooling by the seashore, two rivers down, where you went, once. 'Hark!' Not that. This is real. The sound still there, the soft sough caught behind your fingers. Louder, closer, closer as you get. From waking to dream-time— there, too, along with brides of flowers, silver moon-goddesses, lost heads. The bride running along it—'fast, Blodeuwedd, faster, you and your virgins, hurry, before they catch you'; the goddess rising above it, Arianrhod, silvering, slivering its surface; the heads found within. Up, down, gushhhhhhhhh. Purrrrl. T…rilllll! An accompaniment. Your music.

River birthed, wood raised me.

Cross the river, at the lower ford, much where you were born. Slip between the clefted rock, shed by the mountain, and burrow your way in. Beetle-spread, over or under the fallen trunks, moss-fleeced, fern and fungus pitted, scattering misplaced fairy-hats along the way. Your hand smoothing the fur as you go, wanting to pause, to explore the world beneath it, on the bark of the sycamore, of the beech… but, no—you will wait for the oak for that; the

Oak, the king of the trees (queen, mother—whichever you favour—the 'she' is what *I* favour, now), of the valley, the true mistress of Cynfal, not Cynvael, if you look at it another way, the right way.

You live in its branches now, when you are not beneath the water. You visit the top of the mountains, to look down on this cwm you call home. Or… you gaze at the heavens, your celestial treasure. You might look for Lucy, sure of her soul, sure she is welcomed there, on the brightest of the stars, resting in an ocean of bliss. Or, perhaps, she is a ray of the moon, blessed by its Mother, its light lapping over you.

You will join her in time. For now, you run with Blodeuwedd, the hare, the fox; you fly with the eagle, the raven, the owl. You dance with the maidens, under the Fall, the heads nodding at your play. You swim with the otter, the fish—yes, you have forgiven the fish, it is simply life's/ death's way—tumbling to and fro, watching the trees through River's blear, before you dive, deep, deep, down… to breathe.

You are part of it, you are one with it. Now, and forever. It is where you belong.